JEALOUS
MISTRESS

Susan Alexander

ISBN: 1463503652
ISBN-13: 9781463503659

For Meredith and Leslie
With endless thanks, once again

For Herb
Forever in my heart

"But I will say that [the Law] is
a jealous mistress and requires a
long and constant courtship...."

Remarks by Associate Justice Joseph Story of the United
States Supreme Court, upon his installation as Dane
Professor of Law at Harvard Law School, 1829

CHAPTER 1

Kay Boyer was dead. I was sure of it.

Her body lay in the chest, half-buried by old clothes, blood oozing all over her smart gray flannel dress.

My mind reeled.

I felt dizzy, and my heart was pounding. I turned around and spotted the kid-sized chairs a few feet away. I grabbed one, fell into it, and tried to make sense out of what I had found.

This had always been such a safe, secure place, this classroom in the nursery school. The nursery school Marv and I had selected for our two darling daughters. How had it suddenly become a bloody scene out of a nightmare-inducing movie?

I tried to think. Why would anyone kill Kay Boyer? She was the best nursery school director on the North Shore. Okay, maybe just one of the best. But who would kill a pleasant middle-aged woman who ran a school for three- and four-year-olds?

Clearly, I was out of my depth here. I had to call the police.

A phone, a phone.... Where could I find a phone?

I finally remembered seeing a phone in the supply room. I stood up, shaking, and stumbled out of the classroom toward the phone. My hand trembled while I dialed 911.

"East Winnette Emergency Line," a calm voice said.

Why did I expect the voice to be as shook up as I was?

"I just found a body. A dead body," I said.

"Where are you calling from?"

"East Winnette Nursery School."

"Your name, please?"

"Alison Ross."

"Are you in any danger, Ms. Ross?" the voice asked.

"No...no...I'm all right...I guess."

It hadn't occurred to me that I might be in danger. Maybe I was.

"Please send a car here right away," I said. "I'm scared."

The voice assured me that East Winnette's finest were on their way.

CHAPTER 2

Two hours later I was sitting across a cluttered desk at the East Winnette police station.

I was still shaking.

I'd already told my story twice, to two different middle-aged police officers. Now a young detective with an unusually round face and prematurely gray hair had gone off somewhere to get me a cup of coffee. I figured it was his turn next.

A couple of abandoned ketchup packets sat atop the clutter on his desk. It was October 1981, and the shiny plastic packets reminded me of the latest folly emanating from Washington, D.C.: the Reagan administration had just declared that ketchup was a vegetable.

The detective's office did nothing to relieve the depression that had settled over me. Gray walls, gray metal filing cabinets, gray metal desk and chairs. A relentlessly cold metallic decor. Interior design by U.S. Steel.

My hands were trembling, and I clenched my fists, hoping that would make them stop. With nothing but gray walls to stare at, I tried to think about Marv, the girls, anything but the bloody scene I'd just witnessed.

But I couldn't do it. I couldn't stop thinking about Kay Boyer.

I'd first met Kay Boyer three years before, when my older daughter Missy was about to start school. Marv and I'd heard countless raves about East Winnette Nursery School, and we moved heaven and earth to enroll her there.

Kay Boyer–"Mrs. Boyer" to the children and, by extension, to their parents–had founded East Winnette Nursery School about fifteen years earlier, and she'd headed it ever since. It was a remarkably good nursery school, too, or at least a lot of parents in East Winnette thought so. Every January they fought their way through mounds of snow, then waited in long lines in the school's dank basement to register their little darlings in one of the fall classes. It was almost like applying for entrance to the Ivy League, or some pretentious prep school like North Shore Preparatory, and lots of kids got stuck on the waiting list each year.

I waited in one of those lines that January, and the following September, about a week before Missy started school, a postcard from Mrs. Boyer arrived, telling us the time and place of her first conference with Missy.

But the postcard was sent to Ross Merrill, instead of Merrill Ross (Missy's real name) and it began, "Dear Ross." So I went to the conference expecting Mrs. Boyer to be just short of a half-wit.

But I was wrong.

She was bright and charming, just warm and friendly enough to put Missy at ease without scaring her to death. She was tall and slim, with an abundance of gleaming silver hair and a full, almost sensual mouth. Her obvious intelligence, relaxed manner, and breezy charm—they inspired the confidence you want to have in your child's first teacher. It was easy to see why East Winnette was one of the best nursery schools on the North Shore.

Once Missy started school, I began hearing about Mrs. Boyer's "board." It wasn't a real corporate board of course, just a group of volunteer mothers who carried out Mrs. Boyer's pet projects for the school. The winds of social change had just begun to blow through East Winnette, and boards like these were still made up of nothing but mothers.

The kids' fathers? Most of them were absent from the scene, having clambered on the 7:35 or the 7:54 train to Chicago, arriving at the swank offices of their law firms or multinational corporations before nine o'clock and staying there till well past dinnertime.

We had our share of working mothers in East Winnette—a therapist here, a real estate agent there. But except for a few of the dual-career couples who had begun buying the priciest homes, most of the mothers stayed home with the kids, at least for a while.

Mrs. Boyer was always after me to join "her board," especially when she learned I was an unemployed graduate of Harvard Law School. Truth to tell, I was something of a curiosity: a Harvard-trained lawyer who'd assumed the role of East Winnette housewife and mother for the duration.

I had my reasons. First, there was the crazy path my life had taken after I met Marv. My career had just begun to take off when I met him at a dreary party one Saturday night in L.A. After finishing law school, I'd clerked for a federal judge in Chicago, then taken a job with a mid-sized law firm in Century City.

I admit it: Marv swept me off my feet. He was everything I looked for in a man: good-looking, kind, funny, thoughtful, and off-the charts smart.

He looked a lot like Robert Redford in "Butch Cassidy and the Sundance Kid." He really did.

We discovered at that dreadful party that we had Harvard in common. He'd finished at the college and left for grad school on the West Coast, while I turned up in Cambridge one year later to study law. Once we started talking about good old Harvard, among countless other things, we never stopped.

My job at the law firm was a satisfying combination of courtroom appearances and background research, and I probably would have stayed there for a few more years. But when Marv and I took the plunge and got married, that job got the old heave-ho. Instead of settling in L.A., we moved around the country a couple of times till Marv got a professorship with tenure in Chicago. That's life in academia, folks.

Meanwhile, I got by with some half-baked jobs I scrounged up wherever we happened to be living. Also meanwhile, I twice found myself indulging in the joys of pregnancy, labor, and childbirth.

Now, settled at last in East Winnette, I wasn't working at all. *Outside the home,* that is. And I was more or less reconciled to being a full-time mommy for a while.

Wait a second. "Reconciled" doesn't begin to explain it. I'd made a conscious choice to stay home with my kids.

I'd heard the horror stories: At-home babysitters who watched TV all day, rising from the sofa just long enough to make a high-fat, high-sodium lunch. Day-care centers where kids communicated one variety of virus after another to their little playmates. Babies who didn't recognize their lawyer-mommies at the end of a very long workday and ran to be held by their nannies instead.

I'd rejected that approach to motherhood. Not for everyone, you understand. For me, Alison Ross. Me and no one else. How others chose to live their lives was up to them.

It meant a lot less money, of course. Living on a college professor's salary, Marv and I had to watch our pennies. But I felt this tremendous pull on me, this need to be with my kids. I wanted to be the person molding their little minds. Not somebody else, like a nanny or a day-care worker. The girls seemed to be thriving, and I was certain that my being around all the time was largely responsible.

But there were plenty of days when I wondered whether I really *was* doing the right thing. Some days I even wondered if I'd ever work as a lawyer—or anything else—again. Staying home full-time with your kids can do that to you.

I'd think about some of my classmates, who by this time were partners in high-powered law firms, or judges, even White House pooh-bahs, and I'd get a sinking feeling in my stomach. Would I ever again do anything besides wipe runny noses and read funny little books by Dr. Seuss?

Sure, I'd tried to find a part-time job. But nothing had come along so far. Nobody seemed to want a part-time lawyer. I tried to keep my brain from rotting by watching political commentary on PBS and attacking a towering stack of books after the girls went to bed.

Marv's job as a college professor helped in a way. Although the pay was skimpy, he could do a lot of his work at home, and that gave me some breaks from constant stay-at-home-mom-duty. It was working out, at least for now.

Mrs. Boyer seemed to sense my occasional discomfort with my going-nowhere status and repeatedly tried to recruit me for her board. But I always managed to put her off. The mothers on the board reminded me of some of the sorority girls I'd known in college. Bouncy types with slim bodies, tiny noses, and squeaky clean blond hair fashionably styled in some expensive salon.

Me? I fought a constant battle with my weight, I barely managed to wash my mop of frizzy red hair once a week, and as for noses, mine was far from tiny. Somehow I didn't think I belonged.

Missy's two years at the nursery school zoomed by, and the following fall I found myself accompanying daughter #2 to a conference with Kay Boyer. Lindsay seemed as taken with Mrs. Boyer as Missy had been, and her first year of school went swimmingly. By the fall of her second year, she felt totally at home and began bringing Tammy, her favorite stuffed animal, to school nearly every afternoon.

Tammy. That stupid worn-out stuffed rabbit with one ear. Thanks to Tammy, I was now the lucky person who'd found Kay Boyer, dead as a doornail, lying in a pile of blood-soaked clothes.

CHAPTER 3

I could be creative and blame it on the spaced-out cashier at the supermarket the day before. I got stuck in her check-out line, the slowest on record, and arrived at the nursery school ten minutes past pick-up time. Mrs. Boyer looked annoyed, so I grabbed Lindsay and, mumbling an apology, dashed out.

Back home, Lindsay firmly planted in front of the TV with a plate of granola cookies, we made the awful discovery that Tammy had been left behind at school. Even "Sesame Street" couldn't ease the pain, and Lindsay's wails soon drowned out Big Bird's nasal tones.

"Okay, okay," I said, trying to be heard over the din of the TV and her sobs. "As soon as Missy gets home, we'll go back to school and look for Tammy."

Missy got home from first grade five minutes later, and Lindsay and I dragged her with us to the car. The Toyota's tires squealed as I drove to the nursery school as fast as I could. We pulled up near the entrance and hurried out of the car, but the door was already locked.

Lindsay was inconsolable. Even when Marv came home and, like a good daddy, tried to get her mind off Tammy, he couldn't do it. All through dinner Lindsay sobbed for Tammy. I had to do something, anything, so I decided to call Mrs. Boyer at home and arrange to pick up Tammy at school early the next morning. I was sure Kay Boyer would come through for Lindsay. That was the kind of teacher she was.

Lindsay's brown eyes were still brimming with tears while I dialed the number listed in the school handbook as Kay Boyer's home phone. The phone rang a dozen times. No answer.

I was tempted to hang up, but a quick look at Lindsay's tear-stained face convinced me to wait. After at least twenty rings, someone finally picked up the receiver. A young woman's voice answered.

"May I speak to Mrs. Boyer, please?" I asked.

"Hold on. It's for you, Mom!" the young woman shouted as she put down the receiver, hard.

I heard some scuffling. At last Mrs. Boyer came to the phone.

"Yes?" she said, sounding harassed.

"Mrs. Boyer, it's Alison Ross, Lindsay's mother," I said quickly. "She's in your afternoon class. I'm sorry to bother you at home but...."

"It's quite all right, Mrs. Ross," she said. "What is it?"

"Lindsay left one of her toys at school today, and she's simply miserable without it. Do you think I could meet you at school first thing in the morning and pick it up?"

Mrs. Boyer sighed. "Of course, that'll be fine. Meet me in Lindsay's classroom at quarter to nine. You can pick it up before any of the children in the nine-thirty class arrive."

"Thanks, Mrs. Boyer. That's great." The relief in my voice must have been obvious.

"You're very welcome. I'll see you then." Mrs. Boyer hung up.

I turned triumphantly to Lindsay. "See? Mommy will get Tammy tomorrow morning. You'll have Tammy back by nine o'clock. Now it's time for bed!"

Lindsay finally consented to go upstairs and get into bed without Tammy. Five minutes later she was sound asleep. Missy headed for bed a few minutes later, and I tucked her into bed, too.

I gazed down at my two dark-haired daughters (the red-haired gene had vanished, at least for now). I felt inordinately lucky to have them in my life and headed back downstairs.

Marv was seated on the sofa, immersed in a math journal, one of his favorite preoccupations. Would anyone ever guess that this adorable man had the razor-sharp mind of a math genius?

I know I didn't. The first time I saw Marv, I just thought he was a great-looking guy.

"Can you stick around in the morning while I run over to the nursery school?" I asked.

"My class starts at ten, so you have to be back here by nine at the latest."

"It'll just take a few minutes. It's much easier if I don't have to drag Lindsay along."

"I know, sweetness. But you really need to be back here by nine."

"No problem," I said. "Mrs. Boyer's never late."

CHAPTER 4

The next morning Lindsay was up at seven, demanding to know why I hadn't picked up Tammy yet. I helped Missy get ready for school, then got myself ready to meet Mrs. Boyer. Marv was already looking at his watch when I walked out the door at twenty-five to nine.

"Don't forget, sweetness, I have to leave at nine o'clock," he said.

"I'll be back in fifteen minutes. Don't worry."

"Hurry up, Mommy," Lindsay called after me. An hour and a half of waiting had left her impatient and irritable.

I felt that way, too. I walked quickly through the back yard to the Toyota, swearing to myself that I would never, *never* let her take Tammy to school again.

Once outside, I felt the fog hit me. Thanks to its enviable location on the shores of Lake Michigan just north of Chicago, East Winnette had a beautiful (though eroding) beach, a few enormous homes perched on the lakefront, pretty nice homes almost everywhere else, and lots of foggy mornings in the spring and fall.

Mist covered the windshield of the Toyota, parked outside in the makeshift gravel-covered parking space next to our ancient one-car garage. I cleared the mist with my wipers and drove off.

The nursery school used a small yellow brick building owned by St. Albert's Methodist Church. The church sat on a large corner lot, dwarfing the little building that stood in its shadow. St. Albert's hadn't used the building for years and happily rented it to the school in return for cold hard cash.

When I parked outside the school's entrance five minutes early, I didn't expect the door to be open, but I tried it anyway. It was open. Maybe Mrs. Boyer liked to get to school early.

I entered the building, feeling a bit uneasy. It was almost like entering someone's home without the host's being there.

Inside, it was quiet and dark. No one had turned on the hall lights yet. I found a light switch and turned them on myself. The old-fashioned switch made a loud noise in the early morning silence, startling me.

Calm down, I told myself. Why should I feel nervous here, in my child's nursery school? Still, I did feel unaccountably nervous as I approached Lindsay's classroom through the silent hallway.

As I neared the doorway to the classroom, a young man suddenly appeared in the threshold and strode through it. Again, I was startled, but not for long. He looked familiar. I'd seen him working around the building, emptying wastebaskets and mopping the floors. A husky young man, he'd always struck me as the kind of guy who did his job well enough but had a fairly laid-back approach to it.

His brown hair looked appealingly tousled as he emerged from the classroom. I had to admit that, despite a somewhat prominent jaw, he was a pretty good-looking guy.

I noticed he was sporting a stylish cinnamon suede jacket that didn't quite square with his job of manual worker. He glanced at me and looked surprised to see anyone in the hallway. He brushed by me quickly and left the building through the same door I'd just walked through.

I entered the empty classroom. The lights were on, and I figured the janitor, or whatever he was, must have been cleaning the room before I arrived.

While I waited for Mrs. Boyer, I began to search for Tammy. She wasn't with the dolls in the Doll Corner, and she wasn't in the play kitchen either. I scanned the white wooden bookshelves and looked through the big red boxes where the blocks were stored.

No Tammy. Curious.

I glanced at my watch. Ten minutes to nine. Mrs. Boyer should have been here by now.

I strolled over to the window to look outside for her car, and I found myself leaning over the large chest that was pushed against the wall beneath the window. The chest was a storehouse for the old clothes the children loved to dress up in. Mrs. Boyer wouldn't have put Tammy in there, would she? I'd looked nearly everywhere else, and Marv had to leave for school in the next few minutes.

I couldn't face the prospect of going home without Tammy, so I decided to rummage through the chest.

Carefully opening the lid, I at first saw nothing but the shabby old clothes arranged in the usual haphazard fashion. Looking closer, I spotted the straw hat with the big floppy brim that Lindsay adored. I'd seen her run to grab it when she arrived at school with me just last week.

But the hat looked different now. Hadn't it always been a plain natural straw color? Now it had some large patches of red. A strange shade of red. I reached into the chest and pulled it out.

The red patches were wet, and when I touched them, they made my fingertips red, too. I looked back into the chest.

Under a torn silk scarf and a faded Mexican poncho, a woman's body lay in the midst of the pile of old clothes, blood slowly oozing all over her smart gray flannel dress. It was Kay Boyer, and she was dead. I was sure of it.

CHAPTER 5

The round-faced detective briskly re-entered his office and handed me a styrofoam cup filled with coffee.

"Forgive the delay, Mrs. Ross, but things have been pretty crazy around here. Haven't had a murder in a long time. Everybody's rusty."

I nodded and took a sip of the coffee. Undrinkable. The kind you got in offices where employees made it in a hurry and rarely rinsed out the pot. I wanted to get rid of it as fast as I could.

I thrust the cup towards a stack of papers on the detective's desk. My hands were still shaking, and the coffee cup began to tip over. I grabbed it before its contents landed on his stack.

"Sorry," I muttered, but he hadn't even noticed.

"It took me a while just to review the procedures we all learned for a case like this," he was saying, leafing through a folder. "Hence the delay in going over your statement with you." He flashed a smile at me. "You've become quite an important person, you know. You discovered the body *and* you saw someone leaving the scene of the crime."

"Yes, I know." Jeez, I thought, does he think he needs to tell me I found Kay Boyer's body? I didn't need anyone to tell me that.

Did he think I could forget, could *ever* forget, the sight of her cold white face and her blood oozing all over everything?

"Now, tell me again, this man you saw, you're pretty sure he's a janitor employed by the nursery school?"

"I'm not sure," I said. "But I've seen him around the school a few times, and he was always cleaning up. I can't tell you any more than that."

An image of the husky young man in a cinnamon suede jacket flashed inside my head. I blinked, trying to dislodge it.

"Okay, well, that gives us something to go on, anyway," he said, his cherubic face looking pleased. His voice took on a confidential tone. "You know, this is the first murder we've had in East Winnette in sixteen years."

"Sixteen years?"

"Yeah. We didn't have too much trouble solving that one," he said, as though he had himself been on the force sixteen years before, instead of in, say, third or fourth grade. "It was one of those domestic situations, where the husband killed his wife so he'd inherit her money. They lived in one of those big mansions on Lake Shore Avenue, and the house and most of the money was in her name. But he was a total idiot and really screwed up," he added, smiling. "We got the evidence on him right away."

"How did he do it?" I asked.

"He put cyanide in a pot of coffee he made one morning."

If it had tasted anything like your coffee, I thought, that woman would be alive today.

"Later he even admitted making the coffee," he went on. "He must have thought he'd be okay because he poured it all down the drain. But the moron knew nothing about housekeeping. He forgot to rinse out the pot, and there was enough residue in it to prove he'd killed her. What a fool!" He laughed. "Besides, he had a clear motive. We were on to him right away."

"Whatever happened to him?" I wanted to know more about the East Winnette Coffeepot Murderer.

"He pleaded guilty and went to prison. Died of a heart attack there a few years ago." The detective tried to hold back a smile but failed. It ended up as a smirk. Truth and justice had triumphed in the end, and he was pretty damned happy about it.

Funny, I'd never heard about that murder. I'd never heard about *any* murder in East Winnette. It was the kind of place where, except for an occasional purse-snatching or a Saturday night fist-fight between inebriated teenagers, violent crime occurred exclusively on 27-inch television sets.

"Well, we've got another murder case now." The detective again tried to suppress a smile, but his cherubic face gave him away. It fairly beamed with excitement.

"Do you think the husband did it this time, too?" I asked. I'd never seen or even heard of a Mr. Boyer. I wondered what Kay Boyer's husband was like. A vibrant personality like her, competing with her for dominance in the family circle? Or a quieter, more contemplative type, lurking in the background while she ran the show?

"Oh, no, I doubt it," he said, shaking his head. "The guy's really torn up about it. The officers who went to the house tell me he collapsed when they told him. They're thinking of putting him in the hospital for a couple of days till he pulls out of it. He's a much older guy, and he seems kind of frail. Besides, as far as I know, I don't think he had a motive. The house is in his name. Apparently he inherited it from some relative of his."

Kay Boyer's husband didn't sound like either man I'd pictured. I found it hard to imagine her married to someone old and frail.

"So who do you think did it?" I was genuinely puzzled. Who would want to kill the director of a nursery school?

"Well, it's kind of early to say anything definite, but the guy you saw in the hall, we know he was at the scene of the crime, and it's possible he did it."

"But what was his motive?"

"I'm not sure," he said. "We're checking into his background right now. We're also trying to find the guy, and when we do, we'll take him in for questioning. So we'll just have to wait and see."

"I can't believe he'd have any reason to kill Mrs. Boyer. He just worked around the place."

A doubt entered my mind the minute I said it. He *had* acted suspiciously, the way he brushed past me in the hall. And why was the hallway so dark when I entered if he was supposed to be working there?

"Well, as I said, we'll have to wait and see," the detective said. He got up to signal that our interview was over. I stood up, too. "Now let me thank you again for cooperating with us. I'll be in touch with you if I need any more information. My name is Bob Shakespear."

"Shakespeare?" I asked. "As in Will?"

"Not quite." He picked up the name plate on his desk and turned it toward me. White letters spelled out "ROBERT SHAKESPEAR" on a field of gray vinyl. "We all like to think we're related, even when it's spelled like this. No one knows for sure, of course."

"Of course. But then, 'What's in a name? A rose by any other name would smell as sweet.'"

I felt dumb the minute I said it. It didn't seem right to be flippantly quoting Shakespeare two hours after finding Kay Boyer's dead body. It had to be a crazy reaction to what had happened. Some need for comic relief after the horrible shock at the nursery school.

Bob Shakespear didn't seem upset. He laughed. "Yeah, right. Well, thanks again for your help."

"Sure."

"By the way, my dad likes to think we spell it the right way. Without the "e" on the end. Shake-a-spear, get it? But as far as finding out if we're really related, who knows? My guess is that Will was one of my ancestors, and the "e" got dropped by some half-literate clerk on Ellis Island when my great-grandfather came through."

I nodded. "You're probably right. Those clerks did a number on a lot of people," I said, thinking of my grandfather's friend, Sam Sex. Some clerk must have heard "Sacks" and wrote down "Sex."

Was it meant to be a joke? Or did the name just sound that way to the clerk? Either way, the poor man had to go though life being called "Mr. Sex." I couldn't begin to imagine how awful that must have been.

"Well," Bob Shakespear was saying, "I'll get in touch with you as soon as I know anything else."

"Thanks," I said. "I'm pretty shook up about all this."

"I know," he said.

He offered his hand. I shook it and walked out.

CHAPTER 6

I drove home wondering what Marv would say when I got there. I'd phoned him from the nursery school just after I called the police. "Why not?" he asked when I broke the news that I couldn't be home by nine o'clock.

"Because I just found Mrs. Boyer here, dead."

"Dead? She's dead?"

"You'll have to call the campus and ask them to cancel your ten o'clock class. The police want me to stay here till they arrive, then go to the station for questioning."

The line was silent for a moment. "Right," he said finally, sounding resigned to scheduling a make-up. He hated scheduling make-ups. "Are you okay?"

"Yes…I think so."

"Thank God for that. Well, please try to get home as soon as you can. Maybe I can still make my one o'clock."

Now I looked at my watch as I let myself into the house. It was just after 11:30, and Marv could easily get to his one o'clock on time.

"Hi, honey!" I shouted. I could hear Mr. Rogers singing on the living room TV. He'd keep Lindsay distracted for a while.

Marv found me in the kitchen. Concern for me had wrinkled his forehead. "What happened, sweetness? I've been so worried about you," he said. The irritation of missing his ten o'clock class had clearly subsided. He put his arms around me, and I told him everything that happened.

"Sounds really grim," he said when I finished. He poured a mug of coffee from the carafe on the counter and handed it to me.

"I know. And not only did I find a dead body, but now I also have to entertain Lindsay every afternoon."

"But you don't have to worry about Lindsay," he said, smiling for the first time since I walked in the door. "One of the mothers from the nursery school called. They found someone to fill in for Mrs. Boyer. All her classes will be held at the usual time, starting this afternoon."

"Thank God!" I felt genuinely relieved. "I don't think I could have coped with her this afternoon. Not after this morning."

Marv gave me another hug. "Just give her lunch and take her over there at 12:30, the way you always do." He grabbed his briefcase and ducked out after a quick kiss.

Somehow I got Lindsay through a hasty peanut butter and jelly sandwich, explaining while she ate that Mrs. Boyer was sick and wouldn't be teaching her class any more. She seemed to understand that her frantic demands for Tammy had to take a back seat. I promised we would look for Tammy once we got to school.

As we entered the building, holding hands, I tried not to tremble. I didn't want to frighten Lindsay.

The hallway was dark after the crisp autumn sunshine. As we approached the classroom, I suddenly had an image of the scene that morning, the husky young man in the cinnamon suede jacket brushing past me as he left the room. I felt cold and sick to my stomach.

"Come on, Mommy," Lindsay said, tugging my hand. "We have to look for Tammy."

We entered the classroom, and I quickly glanced around. The police had apparently completed their examination, and mothers and children were filtering in as usual. Only the chest under the window was gone. Someone had put an old rug on the spot where it had been. To cover the bloodstains, no doubt. Some boxes filled with colorful blocks sat on top of the rug to hold it in place.

But what if some little kid looked under the rug?

"Mommy, look!" Lindsay let go of my hand and ran to one of the small arts-and-crafts tables. "Here's Tammy! She's under this table!" Lindsay hugged Tammy to her tiny bosom.

"That's wonderful, darling!" I glanced around the room again. Some of the mothers were clustered together, talking furiously and staring at me. Just then a slight gray-haired woman entered the room with a purposeful look on her face.

"People, people, come to order now," she said in a reedy voice. "It's time for class to begin. My name is Mrs. Thurgood, and I'm going to be your teacher today. I taught at this school a long time ago, and I'm back today because Mrs. Boyer can't be here any more."

She looked disapprovingly around the room. "And now, will the children please come sit on the floor near me, and will the mothers please leave?" She said the last part of the sentence slowly and meaningfully, looking straight at the mothers in the room.

We all left quickly, waving rapid goodbyes to our offspring as we went. Outside, I headed straight for my car.

"Hey, Alison, wait a minute."

I turned and saw Mary Beth Bannister a few yards behind me. I waited for her to catch up. Mary Beth's daughter Jennifer was a friend of Lindsay's, and they sometimes played together at Mary Beth's house.

I liked Mary Beth. She was one of the friendlier mothers at the nursery school. Her long brown hair frizzed like mine in humid weather, and I felt allied to her because of it. It was the two of us up against the bouncy neatly-coiffed blondes.

"Someone said you found Mrs. Boyer's body this morning," she said. "Is that true?"

I nodded. "I was here early this morning to pick up one of Lindsay's toys, and I was supposed to meet Mrs. Boyer. But instead I found...I found her body. In the old-clothes chest, no less." I tried to sound ironic, but what I really felt was nauseated and shaky.

"Want to have a cup of coffee and talk about it?" Mary Beth suggested. Her heart-shaped face lit up at the prospect of getting more inside dope.

"Not really. Maybe another time," I said. "Right now I just want to go home and collapse."

"I understand." Mary Beth's face now registered disappointment mixed with concern. "Well, let me know if I can help," she said.

"Thanks, Mary Beth." I watched her walk toward her station wagon.

I climbed into the Toyota and drove home. Fat golden leaves were blowing through the air and hitting my windshield as they fell from the big old trees that filled East Winnette.

Our crisp autumn afternoons were numbered. In a few weeks, the gray winter days would begin, the trees turning bare and ugly against the somber winter sky.

Dead leaves, dead bodies. I seemed to see death everywhere today.

Back home, I collapsed on the living room sofa and tried to read the morning *Tribune*. But I couldn't concentrate. I was reading the same words over and over without comprehending any of them. After a few minutes I put down the paper, grabbed the phone on the end table, and dialed a familiar number.

CHAPTER 7

"Dickens & Murray," said a cheerful voice on the other end.

"Judy Kerner, please," I said, dying to hear Judy's raspy voice instead.

"Ms. Kerner's out to lunch," the receptionist answered. "Can I take a message?"

Damn it. "Yes, you can. Please tell her Alison called."

"How do you spell that?"

"A-L-I...," I began.

"That's one 'L'?" the voice asked. I'd been asked that question at least six zillion times before.

"Yes, that's one..."

"Oh, just a minute," the voice interrupted. "Ms. Kerner just walked in. Hold on and I'll connect you."

Thank God, I thought. Judy's voice finally came on the line.

"Alison, is that you?"

"I have to talk to you. Do you have a minute?"

"Well, I have a client coming in at 2 o'clock, and a deposition at 4, but I've got a few minutes now. What's up?"

"You won't believe what happened, Judy. I can barely believe it myself."

"Good or bad, Alison?"

"It's...bad."

"Hey, this sounds serious. Are the kids all right? Marv?"

"Oh, yes, everybody's fine. It's not that."

"Well...what is it then?"

"Judy, I found a dead body this morning. Lindsay's teacher. At her school."

"What happened? A heart attack?"

"No, no, it's nothing like that. She...she was murdered... stabbed...with a knife."

"What?"

"She was stabbed, Judy. Stabbed to death."

"You're kidding."

"I wish."

"You mean in safe, safe East Winnette, where nobody's poor?"

"Judy...."

"Where the police just barely manage to justify their existence by busting teenagers for DUI on Saturday night? You're telling me that someone in East Winnette actually got murdered?"

"Yes, Judy, and stop being so goddamned cute about it." I was getting angry. "Have you been listening? I found the body. And it was a bloody mess."

"Okay, okay, Ali. Don't get upset. I'm sorry I said that. It must have been awful for you."

"It was. First I found the body. Then I called the police and waited till they got there. After they showed up, they took me to the station and questioned me."

"God, Ali. They don't suspect you, do they? Did they read you your *Miranda* rights before they questioned you?"

"Oh, Judy, get serious. They don't suspect me."

"Well, who *do* they suspect? Another teacher?"

"No...no. They think the janitor did it."

"The janitor? They think the janitor did it?" Judy burst into laughter. "That's great. It's almost as good as the butler!"

"Judy!"

She was still laughing. "Well, Ali, you have to admit.... I mean, why would the janitor do it? Did he have the hots for her or something?"

"How do I know?" Judy's questions were legitimate, but how should I know what was going on? All I did was discover the body.

Wait a minute. That *wasn't* all.

"Actually, Judy, I saw the janitor leaving the room where I found her."

"What? You saw him?"

"Yep." My hands started to tremble again. Suddenly I wanted to get off the phone and have a drink. Some wine maybe. There was a jug of Inglenook blush in the fridge. "Listen, Judy, I'd better let you go. You sound really busy today."

"Right. I am. But, Ali, let's get together sometime. Maybe I can help you in some way. Classmates have to stick together, right?"

"Right."

"Give me a call tomorrow. Maybe we can meet for lunch this week."

"Okay, sure, Judy. Talk to you then." I hung up.

Talking to Judy hadn't really helped. In a way, I felt more depressed than ever. Judy's life—her big downtown law firm, her posh city apartment on the fringes of Lincoln Park, her glittering friends in the mover-and-shaker world she now inhabited—it seemed like another planet to me, light-years removed from mine.

Was I jealous? Sometimes. But Judy sometimes seemed jealous of me and the life I shared with Marv and the girls.

Every time we talked, an awkward silence eventually arose, separating us, reminding us what different paths we'd taken.

Still, that old bond—struggling through three years of law school together—always brought us together again. I felt closer to Judy than I felt to any of my friends in East Winnette.

Right now all I wanted was that pale pink liquid in the fridge. I poured myself half a tumblerful and curled up on the sofa. A few minutes later, the wine producing a lovely haze, I pulled an old afghan over me and fell asleep.

* * *

I was jerked awake by a loud ringing. The phone sat accusingly on the end table.

I was still half-asleep as I reached for it. "Hello?" I said groggily.

"Mrs. Ross?" a reedy voice inquired. "This is Mrs. Thurgood at the nursery school. It's ten minutes past three, and Lindsay is waiting for you to pick her up."

"Oh, my God, I'm sorry," I stammered. "I fell asleep. I'll…I'll be right there."

"Very well, I'll wait for you, but you mustn't let this happen again. I'm very strict about promptness."

"Yes," I said. "You should be. I won't let it happen again."

"Well, hurry over now. Lindsay and I are quite anxious."

I ran to get my jacket and keys, then remembered that Missy was due home from first grade any minute. I usually tried to pick her up on my way home from the nursery school. But on days like this, when for some reason I couldn't pick her up, she walked home from school with the other kids on our block, getting home in about ten minutes.

I peered through the living room window and glimpsed Missy, by herself, slowly strolling down the block toward our house, stopping to pick up autumn leaves as she walked. The other kids must have headed straight for home, leaving her to pursue her fascination with the leaves.

Missy's artistic creativity and scientific curiosity were not traits I treasured at that moment. I ran to the front door and opened it fast. "Hurry up, Missy!" I shouted. "We have to pick up Lindsay right away."

Missy had to go with me to the nursery school. There was no other option. I never left either daughter alone in the house. I'd been spooked by stories of mothers going to the corner store and coming home to find five children burned to death in a fire.

"Pick up Lindsay?" Missy asked as she ran up the front steps. "Isn't she home already?" Her little face looked bewildered.

"No, sweetheart," I said. I tried to be a patient mommy and explain everything. "I fell asleep and forgot to get her at three o'clock. We have to go right now."

"But I'm hungry, Mommy. Can't I eat something first?"

"No!" I said, losing whatever patience I had left. "First we get Lindsay, then you eat. Let's go!"

We arrived at the nursery school as fast as the Toyota could get there. Lindsay and Mrs. Thurgood were waiting just outside the entrance.

Thank goodness I don't have to go inside again, I thought. I pulled up opposite the entrance, and Mrs. Thurgood escorted Lindsay to the car.

"Now, remember, Mrs. Ross. You must be on time in the future," she cautioned as Lindsay climbed into the car.

"Please forgive me. I'm really sorry," I said.

She leaned towards the car as I strapped Lindsay into her car seat. "I know you're under a strain today, my dear," she confided in a softer, more reassuring voice. "I'll overlook it this time. Just make very sure it doesn't happen again."

Her gray curls quivered as she shook her head from side to side, and her index finger pointed at me just as it must have pointed at the generations of students she'd reprimanded over the years.

"I won't, I promise," I muttered, driving off.

Back home, Lindsay (now clutching Tammy) curled up on the sofa to watch "Sesame Street." How did parents survive before PBS? Missy had a snack, then headed for the backyard to search for more autumn leaves.

I got busy fixing dinner—spaghetti, with sauce straight from a jar (one of my specialties), and a salad. A gourmet cook I'm not, never have been, and never will be. At least I never pretended to be much of a cook before Marv and I got married (I'm a firm believer in truth-in-advertising). The most ambitious dish I prepared for him when we were dating was a dazzler from the *I Hate to Cook Book*.

So most nights we all settled for pretty boring fare, like spaghetti, meatloaf, and broiled chicken. I was terrific at baked apples, and I made a mean roast turkey, but otherwise I was no great shakes in the kitchen. Marv was the gourmet cook in our household, preparing his favorite recipes whenever he could find the time.

Marv arrived home, and we all sat down for dinner. Somehow the spaghetti and salad got eaten. After we read some storybooks to the girls, they went off to bed at a decent hour.

Marv and I were finally alone in the living room. "How are you doing, sweetness?" he asked. "You've had a pretty rotten day, haven't you?"

"It *was* rotten. I think I'll head upstairs and go to bed. Try to forget everything that's happened. Maybe when I wake up, things won't seem so awful."

"Sounds like a great idea," he said. "A good night's sleep always helps." He kissed me gently on the lips. I looked into his beautiful gray-green eyes and said goodnight.

But when I got to bed, I couldn't fall asleep. I kept thinking about that morning—the mist on my car, the silent dark hallway, the cinnamon suede jacket, the blood....

Everything whirled around in my mind for what seemed like hours.

I heard Marv come to bed, quietly climbing under the covers so he wouldn't wake me, and after a few minutes I heard his gentle snoring. The clock on my nightstand said midnight, then two, then three. I finally fell asleep, hoping desperately as I dozed off that the images of that morning would be gone when I woke up.

CHAPTER 8

The next morning I awoke feeling almost normal. The usual breakfast busy-ness and getting Missy off to school on time kept me from thinking too much about what had happened the day before. Marv had no classes to rush off to and offered to stay home with Lindsay, but I had laundry piled high in the basement and told him he might as well go to the library to work on his research in relative quiet while I stayed home.

Lindsay was working on a puzzle, and I was in the basement separating the light- and dark-colored laundry, when I heard the phone ring. We didn't have an answering machine (nobody did), and Lindsay was an unreliable phone-answerer, so I madly dashed up the basement stairs. Luckily, the caller was still there when I breathlessly picked up the receiver.

"Mrs. Ross? Bob Shakespear, East Winnette police." I had an immediate mental picture of his cherubic face on the other end of the line. "Just thought I'd let you know what's happening. We tracked down the janitor, and we're charging him with murder. Thanks again for helping us connect him to the crime. We never could have made the arrest so quickly without your help."

"I was glad to help," I said. I felt a bit uneasy with the news. "What makes you so sure he's involved?"

"Well, we got a sheet on him, and he's got a record. Drug-dealing. Never been convicted, but arrested a couple times, and the Chicago police are sure he's a dealer. We think he took this job at the nursery school as a cover while he tried to make new contacts up here on the North Shore."

Nice. A drug-dealer working at the nursery school. "But how does that connect him to Kay Boyer's murder?"

"He was there, Mrs. Ross. You *saw* him. By the way, you'll have to come to the station to identify him before we send him over to Cook County Jail. Can you make it here this morning?"

"Can it wait till this afternoon, after 12:30? Otherwise, I'd have to bring my daughter along." I didn't relish the idea of dragging Lindsay with me to the police station.

"Uh...yeah, I guess so." Mention of a child seemed to throw him. Had he forgotten that the murder took place in a nursery school? "Just be sure you get here by two o'clock. We want to send him over sometime this afternoon."

"Wait," I said. "I still don't see how you connect him to the murder, even if I *did* see him there. That's not enough, is it?" My recollection of criminal law wasn't whiz-bang, but I knew you needed a whole lot of evidence to prove a crime beyond a reasonable doubt.

Shakespear hesitated. "Well, he hasn't confessed yet, but we figure Kay Boyer found out about his drug-dealing and threatened to tell us about it. He got excited and killed her. We found a knife on him that looks like it could be the murder weapon."

"A knife?" I asked, feeling sick to my stomach again, remembering all that blood.

"Yeah," he said. "The medical examiner thinks she was stabbed by some sort of fixed-blade knife. There's this big knife wound in her chest. The wound isn't neat, though, so we can't tell precisely what kind of knife did it. Not yet anyway. Apparently this guy made a mess of the wound pulling it out."

I felt really sick now. "I've got to go," I said quickly. "I'll see you later at the station."

"Yeah, okay. No, wait," he added. "I might not be here then. Just tell reception you're here to identify Jack Hines. That's the guy's name."

I hung up and stood by the phone for a minute, trying to calm down. I couldn't help thinking of Kay Boyer, lying helpless in Lindsay's classroom while Jack Hines, or whatever his name was, twisted and pulled on his knife, trying to get it out of her chest.

"Mommy! Are you there?" Lindsay called from the living room.

"Yes, honey. I'm here, in the kitchen. Be there in a minute." I couldn't face the basement anymore. I didn't want to leave Lindsay alone, or be alone myself, right now. I opened the refrigerator, grabbed a can of Diet Pepsi, and poured myself a tall one.

Thank God for Diet Pepsi, I thought. It's gotten me through some rough times.

I glanced at the clock. Only ten o'clock, but what the hell. Drinking Diet Pepsi at ten a.m. wasn't such a terrible indulgence.

After all, I thought, some people start swilling booze at ten o'clock in the morning. Like my neighbor Martha Murphy. She had the scent of booze on her breath no matter what time of day I ran into her. At least I usually stuck to Diet Pepsi.

Lindsay was in the living room, building a zoo out of small wooden blocks. Her collection of tiny plastic animals was destined to go inside the tiny block cages as soon as she finished constructing them. I helped her with her zoo for a while, then we sat and read some books together. Two of her favorites by Dr. Seuss. About eleven o'clock the phone rang again.

"May I please speak to Mrs. Alison Ross?" the voice inquired.

"Yes."

"Mrs. Ross, my name is Art Jacoby. I'm a reporter at the *Tribune*. We just heard you helped solve a murder in East Winnette. Is that correct?"

"Well, I don't know that I exactly helped solve a murder," I hedged, my heart suddenly thumping again. "I did find...the body, and...and I simply told the police that I saw...I saw a man leaving the room where I found it," I managed to get out.

That was the truth; there didn't seem to be any reason why I couldn't say that much.

"And the man you saw leaving was the janitor, Jack Hines?"

"Well, that's the name the police told me," I said. "I only know I recognized him as someone I'd seen cleaning up around the school."

"Did you know he has a criminal record, that he's suspected of being a drug-dealer?" Jacoby asked.

"That's what the police tell me. I know nothing about it myself." I felt vaguely harassed. The reporter seemed nice enough, but he was starting to push me kind of hard.

"Tell me a little bit about yourself, Mrs. Ross. Are you a housewife, or do you work, or what?"

"Well, I don't think of myself as a housewife," I answered. He was beginning to irritate me. "At the moment I'm a full-time mother because I choose to be, but I'm trained as a lawyer, and I worked as a lawyer before I had my children. Besides, what I do now *is* work. Taking care of children is a full-time job."

"I'm sure you're right about that," he said placatingly. "But you say you were a lawyer?"

"I *am* a lawyer. I'm just not working as a lawyer right now."

"Right. But what I'm getting at is, what did you do when you worked as a lawyer? For starters, where did you go to law school?"

"Harvard."

"Harvard?" Somehow I knew that his eyebrows had just shot up. Harvard usually did that to people.

"Yes. And I held several jobs after law school, starting with a clerkship to a federal judge."

"Which judge?" he asked.

"Richard J. Johanssen," I said, casually dropping the name of one of Chicago's best-known federal judges.

"Johanssen? The guy who ran the Toby Cartwright trial?" Jacoby sounded excited. This phone call had turned out to be a lot more interesting than he'd expected.

"That's right. Although I wasn't his clerk during the Cartwright trial."

"Oh." He sounded a bit deflated. "Well, anyway, you sound like a very interesting woman. I'd like to come out to talk to you in person."

"Well, I...," I began.

"Mommy! Mommy! Get off the phone!" Lindsay suddenly demanded. She came closer and started shouting in my ear. "Hang up! Hang up! Hang up!"

"Stop it, Lindsay! I'm trying to talk to someone!"

"Hang up! Hang up!" she yelled, trying to get the phone away from me. She wanted Mommy back. And she didn't want to share.

"Mr. Jacoby," I began.

"It's Art. Call me Art."

"Okay, Art. Listen, I can't talk right now. If you want more information, talk to Bob Shakespear at the East Winnette police station. He knows a lot more about this than I do."

I was trying to hang onto the phone long enough to say a respectable goodbye.

"Okay," Art said. "Thanks for your help. I'll be in touch."

He and I both said goodbye.

Lindsay hugged me. "Thanks, Mommy," she said sweetly.

I hugged back.

CHAPTER 9

That afternoon I went to the police station to identify Jack Hines. Bob Shakespear wasn't there, but another officer hastily got a line-up together, and I picked out the nursery school janitor right away. He was still wearing the cinnamon suede jacket.

Somehow I got through the rest of the day. Things seemed to be falling into place again. Marv and I took the kids out for dinner at McDonald's—the posh one in Kenilwood, where the gleaming chandeliers and the leafy ferns in hanging ceramic planters almost made you forget you were eating fast food.

While we ate, I looked around. In their Ralph Lauren polo shirts, Banana Republic khakis, and Sperry Top-siders, most of the Kenilwood customers looked as though they'd taken a wrong turn on their way to the country club. I was wearing my washed-out jeans and my faded Harvard sweatshirt and prayed I wouldn't see anyone I knew.

I was in luck. The only people I recognized were the Lerners, who lived across the alley from us. In a Wash. U. sweatshirt that was even grubbier than mine, and with McDonald's special sauce all over her face, Carole Lerner looked as bad as I did. I felt grateful for small favors.

Back home, the kids behaved reasonably well and got to bed without much fuss. I went to bed myself at the usual time and got almost the usual amount of sleep. Maybe life was returning to normal after all.

The next morning Marv had his ten o'clock class again. Before he left, he walked Missy to the corner, then brought in the *Tribune* that was sitting on our front lawn. He wanted to check the ads for new tires, he said, and turned quickly to the sports section. I casually glanced at the front page.

A small headline toward the bottom of the page caught my eye. "SUBURBAN WOMAN IDENTIFIES SUSPECT." My heart started pounding. "Marv, look, there's something in the paper about the murder," I said.

"What?" Marv reluctantly looked up from the sports section. "Something about the murder? What does it say?"

"I don't know yet, I haven't read it, but I think it mentions me," I said.

"You? How did they find out about you?"

"From the police, I guess. A reporter called me yesterday."

"A reporter? You didn't tell me." A wounded look spread across Marv's face.

"I forgot to tell you, honey. I really did."

Marv smiled a forgiving smile and looked back at the latest news about the Bears.

I started to read the article. It was all there: details of the murder, background on the nursery school, a brief sketch of Jack Hines, and a short profile of me, the "suburban woman" who'd identified him. Art Jacoby hadn't left anything out. He'd even mentioned Judge Johanssen and the Toby Cartwright trial.

"Are you finished yet?" Marv asked. "Can I see it?"

I handed the paper to Marv. He scanned the article, then nodded his head approvingly. "Not bad," he said. "A nice write-up about you, Alison."

"Do you think so?" I wasn't so sure. I didn't know whether I wanted everyone in East Winnette to know that much about me. But apparently I didn't have any choice.

Marv gave me a warm corn-flakes-and-coffee-scented kiss and took off for his class. A minute later I got a phone call inviting Lindsay to play at a classmate's house. The mother who called didn't mention the murder. Either she hadn't seen the *Tribune* yet or she was too tactful to broach the subject. Gratefully I dropped off Lindsay and headed for the supermarket.

My friendly neighborhood Jewel was crowded with the usual assortment of shoppers. I looked around, hoping I wouldn't run into anyone who'd read the front page of the *Tribune* that morning.

Out of the corner of my eye I saw Maggie Larson, another mother from the nursery school. I averted my eyes in hopes of avoiding her. I'd once told her about a mind-blowing sale at one of the local kids' clothing boutiques, and she ran off to seek out clothes for her son Nicky. When I saw her again two days later, she told me she'd found some great stuff for him. "I didn't have enough money to pay for them," she added, "but I wanted them, so I just wrote a check. It'll bounce, of course, but I'll worry about that later."

I was shocked to hear Maggie brazenly confide her cavalier approach to "paying" for merchandise she wanted, and I steered clear of her after that. Meanwhile, I pitied the local retailers who had to deal with customers like Maggie.

Now I had to focus on filling up my grocery cart. My fellow shoppers were gliding up and down the aisles of the Jewel, picking items off shelves to the tune of "The Twelfth of Never." The produce section was jammed full of carts, shoppers pinching the apples for crispness, fondling the romaine to make sure it was fresh. I was bored out of my mind, as usual, and checked out as fast as I could. When I got home, the phone was ringing.

I dropped my grocery bags on the kitchen floor and grabbed the phone.

"Is this Mrs. Ross?" a woman's voice asked.

"Yes."

"My name is Elmira Hines," she said. Her voice was gravely, as though she smoked a pack or three a day.

"Yes?"

"I'm Jack's mother. Jack Hines."

I suddenly had a sinking feeling in my stomach. I didn't need a call like this right now, just when things had returned to quasi-normal.

"I read about you in the *Tribune* this morning." She paused. I didn't say anything, so she went on.

"Jack's innocent, Mrs. Ross," she said. "I know you saw him that morning, but he didn't kill her. He told me he didn't."

"Mrs. Hines," I began, "you're his mother. Naturally...."

"Sure, I'm his mother. But he's innocent." She sounded like the kind of mother who is bewildered by a child who's gone wrong, the kind of mother who wants to believe he hasn't gone wrong at all. "You gotta believe me," she said. "He was there, sure. He went to get his jacket. See, he left it there the day before."

"His jacket?" I pictured the cinnamon suede jacket he was wearing that morning at the nursery school, the one he wore in the line-up at the police station.

"Yeah," she said. "He paid a lot for that jacket, and he didn't want to leave it sitting there where the kids could get a hold of it. But he didn't even see Mrs. Boyer. He didn't even see her." She paused again. I didn't say anything.

"Why would he kill her anyways?" she asked. "She was always real nice to Jack. She knew he had some problems with the cops, but she said she'd give him a chance, she'd let him work there if he promised to stay out of trouble."

"Why are you calling *me*, Mrs. Hines?"

"Because you told the police he was there, and now they think he killed her," she said. "Maybe he got into drugs again, he didn't do what he promised, but she didn't know that. And he wasn't gonna let her find out. He never did drug deals near the school. He's not dumb."

"I still don't see what I can do." This call was making me nervous. "I saw him there, and that's all I told the police. I never said he killed her. I don't know who killed her, so I can't accuse him or anyone else."

"But they found a knife on Jack, and now they're pinning this thing on him," she said. "You gotta help him, Mrs. Ross. If it wasn't for you, they never would've gotten on to him."

"They certainly would have," I retorted. "He was working at the nursery school. Don't you think they would have questioned him?"

"Maybe," she conceded. "But maybe he wouldn't have stuck around that long. Jack, he's no dummy. He'd figure out they'd finger him. He'd leave town. But see, when you told them you saw Jack, they got on to him right away. So you're responsible, Mrs. Ross." She paused again.

I said nothing. She had no right to make accusations like this. I only told the police what I saw.

She must have sensed my anger. "Listen, I don't mean to make you mad. All I'm saying is Jack's innocent. He's accused of murder. My son's accused of *murder*. He could get the chair for this. And he didn't do it."

I still said nothing. I was too upset to tell her that Illinois didn't use the electric chair anymore.

"The paper says you're a lawyer," she said. She didn't give up easily. "It says you went to Harvard, and you worked for a judge. You're a smart lady. You can help my Jack, you can prove he's innocent."

"I can't help him, Mrs. Hines. I'm a lawyer, sure, but I'm at home with my kids right now. I don't have an office or a staff or anything. I don't have time to go out and research his case. He needs a practicing lawyer to represent him, someone who's in practice right now. Didn't the police get a lawyer for him?"

"Yeah, they brought in some public defender for him. Jack says he's just a kid, he don't know his backside from his law degree. Oh,...I'm sorry, I shouldn't have said that," she added quickly.

"Listen, that public defender will do a good job. Most public defenders are very good lawyers."

"Maybe." Mrs. Hines sounded dubious. "In the meantime, can you help me? Can you try to find out more about Mrs. Boyer?" she pleaded. "You live out there. You can talk to people who knew her. Maybe something will turn up."

"I'm sure the police have talked to everyone already. What can I find out that they haven't?"

"The police have made up their minds, Mrs. Ross. They think Jack did it, so they're not pushing too hard anymore. But Jack didn't do it!" She paused. "You're a mother. Any mother's gotta understand how I feel. I want my boy out of jail."

"Well, I'll think about it." I tried to sound noncommittal, but her plea had begun to get to me. Especially the part about being a mother. "In the meantime, tell Jack to cooperate with his lawyer. He'll get Jack off if he didn't do it."

"Yeah, sure." Mrs. Hines sounded defeated. "Well, thanks, Mrs. Ross. Whatever you can do, I'll sure appreciate it. I gotta go now."

I hung up, feeling awful. What if Jack Hines was innocent? My placing him at the scene of the crime *had* implicated him. It was purely circumstantial, so was the knife, but combined with his criminal record, they made a pretty good case against him.

I put away the groceries, then headed for the basement laundry room. As I measured the Tide and poured it into my medium-price-range Maytag, I couldn't stop thinking about Jack Hines. If he was innocent, I was, at least in part, responsible for his arrest—and his possible conviction. Could I live with that?

I flipped the dial, and the washer chugged into action. Don't be melodramatic, Alison, I told myself.

But what if he *was* innocent?

I walked upstairs and picked up the phone. Mary Beth Bannister answered after the first ring.

"Hi, Mary Beth. It's Alison Ross."

"Oh, hi, Alison."

"Listen, Mary Beth, you're on the nursery school board, aren't you?" I remembered hearing that Mary Beth had joined the board. The lone member with frizzy hair.

"Yes," she answered. "Why?"

"I'd like to talk to the president of the board." I tried to sound casual. "Can you tell me who it is?"

"Sure. It's Andrea Lewis. But why do you want to talk to Andrea? Is it something to do with the murder?"

"No, not really," I lied. "My neighbor wants to know something about the school, and with Mrs. Boyer gone, I thought I'd ask Andrea."

"Wait, maybe I can help you," Mary Beth said. "I go to all the board meetings, so I know everything that's going on." I could tell she was hoping I'd spill my guts. But I couldn't see getting any real information out of Mary Beth. She was just a shade too ditsy.

"Thanks anyway, Mary Beth. But I really think I should talk to Andrea."

"Okay," she said resignedly. "But if you can't reach her, you might try getting in touch with Rella Cox. The assistant director. She probably knows more about the school than Andrea."

Mary Beth wasn't so ditsy after all. I'd totally forgotten about Rella Cox. "Thanks, Mary Beth. Talk to you later."

I looked up Andrea Lewis's phone number and started dialing.

CHAPTER 10

Andrea didn't answer the first time I called, but when I tried again a half-hour later, she did.

"This is Alison Ross," I began. "I'm one of the mothers from the nursery school, and I was...."

"Oh, I know who you are," Andrea interrupted. "You found Kay Boyer's body, didn't you? I was just reading about you in the *Tribune*."

"That's why I'm calling," I said. "If you're not too busy this afternoon, I'd like to talk to you about Kay Boyer. It'll only take a few minutes."

"Well, I do have an appointment at the hairdresser's at one o'clock," she said. My suspicions about the board members' hair were confirmed. "But if it'll only take a few minutes...."

"I can leave right away." It was almost noon, but Lindsay was having lunch at her classmate's and going to school from there.

"Well, all right. Do you have my address?"

"Sure." It was right there in the school directory, just above her phone number. "I'll be there in a minute or two."

Andrea Lewis lived on one of the most sumptuous blocks in East Winnette—Oak Avenue between 11ᵗʰ and 12ᵗʰ Streets. It was only a few blocks from my house, but those few blocks made all the difference in the world.

The houses on my block ran the gamut from ordinary and somewhat cramped (mine) to large and fairly impressive (the

one next door, belonging to our neighbor, Belinda Copeland).
But the houses on Andrea's block were borderline mansions.
One of them always reminded me of an art museum I once saw
in Williamstown, Massachusetts (on a slightly smaller scale, of
course).

Marv and I'd been lucky to find a house we could afford
in pricey East Winnette. By chance, we'd come across a kindly
real estate agent who moved heaven and earth to track down a
house for us. She finally learned about a two-story fixer-upper
in a great location—near the lake, downtown East Winnette,
and the nearby elementary school. It was owned by an aging
widow who couldn't climb the stairs anymore and was eager to
sell it ASAP. With all its flaws, the house was still a bargain.
We grabbed it and never looked back.

I was hoping Andrea's house would turn out to be the
museum lookalike, but it wasn't. It just looked like one of those
houses in a Cadillac ad in the latest issue of LIFE magazine.

I pulled into Andrea's circular driveway and parked the
Toyota. If a car can look embarrassed, the Toyota did. I rang the
doorbell and waited for Andrea to answer.

"Hi," she said breezily as she opened the door. She was a
striking blonde who could easily grace the cover of *Vogue.* "You
must be Alison. Come on in." She ushered me into a front room
the size of my entire first floor. "Now tell me why you're here."

Andrea seated herself on a chintz-covered loveseat and
indicated that I should sit on its twin. She had an attentive
look on her model-perfect face.

Feeling frumpy in last year's jeans jacket in the middle of
House Beautiful, I sat down and started talking. "As you know,
I found Mrs. Boyer's body at the nursery school, and I also saw
the janitor leaving just as I came in."

"Umm…." Andrea nodded her head.

"Well, now the janitor's been arrested for the murder." She nodded again. "But he claims he didn't do it and...and that I'm responsible for his arrest."

A perplexed look crossed Andrea's otherwise flawless face. "So?" she asked.

"So now I'm wondering whether there might be someone else who could have done it."

"And you think I might know that someone else?"

"Well, you did get to know Mrs. Boyer pretty well, didn't you? As president of the board, I mean," I said.

"Well...yes and no," Andrea reflected. "My contact with Kay was pretty much confined to nursery school business, and Lord knows that kind of thing doesn't tend to arouse anyone's passions." She laughed. "Of course, there was that dispute with Rella Cox over selling the school to Kidd's Korner," she added. Her forehead wrinkled as she said it.

"Kidd's Korner? What's that?"

"Haven't you heard of Kidd's Korner?" My ignorance appeared to amaze Andrea. "It's a chain of day-care centers. They started in California, and now they're all over the country. The chain is run by Gabriel Kidd, a really dynamic guy, or at least that's what Kay told me. He contacted her sometime last year about making the nursery school part of his chain."

"And...?"

"And she took his proposal pretty seriously. She discussed it with Rella and with all of us on the board, but even though most of us opposed it, she was leaning in favor of going with Kidd's Korner."

"She was?" I had no idea Kay Boyer had contemplated any changes at the nursery school. I guess I thought it would go on forever just the way it always had.

"She sure was," Andrea said. "She stood to make a pretty big profit, I think. Gabriel Kidd has lots of bucks, and Kay said he was anxious to make his presence known on the North Shore. So he was willing to pay her a load of cash to move into East Winnette."

"And Rella Cox was opposed to the idea?"

Andrea nodded. "She saw it as a real threat to her position. I think she always expected to take over the nursery school when Kay retired, and Kay had been hinting about retiring for a year or so. But when Kidd's Korner came along, Rella saw herself being booted out."

"Would she really have been fired?" I asked.

"Who knows? I haven't the foggiest idea what Kidd's Korner would have done. Rella probably didn't either. But it was the uncertainty of it that worried her. She'd invested a dozen or so years in the nursery school, and she'd antici-pated taking it over. She was upset, and I can understand why."

"So can I."

Andrea glanced at her watch. "I really must run. But you know, I think you should give Rella a call. You might want to get her point of view."

"Thanks, Andrea. You've been a big help," I said, extract-ing myself from the depths of the loveseat.

Andrea and I walked toward the front door, passing a china cabinet filled with exquisite Lladró figurines. I felt like a chubby-cheeked Hummel figurine next to Andrea, a swan-like Lladró.

"Glad I could help, Alison. Let me know what you find out." Andrea dazzled me with a million-dollar smile. "Bye now."

I walked down the driveway and climbed into the Toyota. Andrea Lewis really had been a big help. Kidd's Korner, Rella Cox, a controversy over becoming part of a national chain—all of it was news to me. Maybe there was more to Kay Boyer's death than a janitor in a cinnamon suede jacket.

CHAPTER 11

I got home about a quarter to one, greeted by a kitchen sink filled with the dirty dishes I'd been trying to ignore since lunch the day before.

Somebody had to load the dishwasher, and I knew that somebody was me.

I reluctantly began to empty the dishwasher, taking the clean dishes out so I could put the dirty ones in. God, I hate this, I thought. Maybe I should look for a full-time job and hire a housekeeper to do all this stuff.

It was a thought that crossed my mind, oh, about thirty-nine times a day.

But then I thought about leaving the house at seven every morning and not getting home till eight at night, and never seeing my kids except at breakfast, bedtime, and occasional weekends, and I knew I just couldn't do it. These years with them were too important; I'd miss too much. My career would just have to wait.

Too bad a math professor's salary didn't allow me to be a full-time mother and have some household help, too.

The ideal, of course (I thought for the millionth time) would be a good part-time job. Working part-time would enable me to keep my career going and have enough money to hire some help. I didn't need a BMW or the latest electronic gizmos to make me happy. Just a few extra bucks so someone could spell me in the laundry room now and then.

The intellectual stimulation would help, too, of course. I adored my kids, and I wanted to be with them most of the time, but total immersion in a law library for a few hours every week would be, well, bliss. I had to admit I missed it.

But the law, they taught us at Harvard, is a "jealous mistress." The dean's welcoming address at orientation made that clear. Lawyers were expected to put their careers first. If you didn't prostrate yourself at the feet of your "mistress," attending to her every whim, you couldn't possibly be a great lawyer.

In other words, you were supposed to devote your every waking moment to the law. At least the old codgers who ran the law firms thought so. They couldn't seem to get it through their heads that part-time employees are far more productive than overworked wage-slaves. So instead of hiring promising applicants who wanted to have some balance in their lives, the law-firm pooh-bahs insisted on hiring bright young lawyers who were willing to work 60 or 80 hours a week.

I'd tried to get a part-time job. Heaven knows I'd tried. But the Harvard placement office was no help. Neither were my law school classmates. Even Judy. I'd asked her repeatedly about doing part-time work at her firm, and each time I did, she'd dutifully talk to the hiring partner, then get back to me with the same old apologies. "They just won't consider part-time here, Ali. Sorry."

It was the same story at all the other firms I contacted. Even the public-interest law offices weren't interested. Okay, I hadn't called every law office in Chicago, but being rejected over and over got depressing after a while. So I pretty much gave up trying.

I knew it was my crazy career path that hindered my finding something. If I'd worked full-time at one job for a bunch of years before I had my kids, I'd have had some stature at my workplace, a niche that would have allowed me to negotiate for part-time. A few women lawyers had begun to do that. But my cross-country moves, happening just when I was having my kids, had made that impossible.

Then there was the notion of sharing a job with another part-time lawyer: that struck me as ideal. But I hadn't heard of any firms or offices willing to experiment with that idea, and I hardly knew how to begin proposing it myself.

That "jealous mistress" bit really got to me, though. What a crock. I finally decided they could keep their jealous mistress, at least for now. I had my kids. And Missy and Lindsay were more important to me than anything else I could think of.

The dishwasher was empty now, but I just couldn't face loading the dirty dishes. I decided to let them soak some more and call Rella Cox instead.

I remembered that she never taught afternoon classes, spending that time on administrative duties and counseling parents of problem children. The word was that Kay Boyer preferred teaching and had chosen to maintain a full teaching schedule while Ms. Cox (unlike Kay Boyer, she called herself "Ms.") taught mornings only and tended to administration.

I looked up the nursery school number and dialed it. "East Winnette Nursery School," a brisk voice answered.

"Is this Ms. Cox?"

"Yes, it is. Can I help you?" She sounded crisply professional.

"This is Alison Ross. My daughter Lindsay is a student at the nursery school. I was wondering if I could come in to see you."

"I wasn't aware that Lindsay was having any problems, Mrs. Ross. She appears to be a very well-adjusted child."

"No, Lindsay's fine. I want to talk to you about something else."

"Something else? You're not soliciting for some charity project, are you?"

"Oh, no. This is strictly about the nursery school. Do you have a few minutes this afternoon?"

"Well, let me check my schedule." I heard her shuffle some papers. "I think I can see you in about half an hour. Will that be all right?"

"Yes, yes, that'll be fine," I said quickly. "I'll be over at 1:30."

"Very good, Mrs. Ross. I'll see you then."

I loaded the dishwasher with the dirty dishes, threw some more laundry into the washing machine, and set out for the nursery school.

Thanks to the felt hat whose car was ahead of me most of the way, I was almost late. Felt hats drove me crazy.

Felt hats? That's what I called elderly male drivers who invariably drove ten miles below the speed limit and wore the felt fedoras that went out of style about the time Eisenhower left office. Whenever I found myself behind one of them, my heart sank. I knew it would take me twice as long to get where I was going.

It was a minute or two past 1:30 when I knocked on the door of Ms. Cox's office. "Come in!" she called.

The office was immaculate, just as I expected. The only evidence that we were in a nursery school was a brightly-colored picture signed "Joshua" that was tacked to a bulletin board on one wall.

Rella Cox waved me into a straight-backed wooden chair opposite her desk. Her pinstriped skirt-suit struck me as an

odd choice for a nursery school setting, and her Dutch boy hair-
cut looked incongruous on her aging narrow face. Was she trying to look stern, hoping parents would think she was tough as
nails? If so, she'd accomplished her goal.

"Sit down, Mrs. Ross. Now what is this all about?" She
pasted a thin-lipped smile on her totally-void-of-makeup face.

"It's about Mrs. Boyer."

"Oh." The thin-lipped smile vanished. "What about
her?"

"Well," I began, "as you may know, I found her body here
at the nursery school."

She nodded.

"I saw Jack Hines leaving just before I found her. I told
the police, and now they've arrested him for her murder. But
I'm not sure he did it."

Her face was stony. "I don't see any reason to discuss this
with you, Mrs. Ross," she said coldly.

I blinked, uncertain what to say next. "Uh…I know you
don't have to talk to me, Ms. Cox. But I feel somewhat responsible for the way things are…."

"Exactly what are you saying?" she interrupted.

My heart started racing. How could I get any information
out of this woman? "I guess I need to explain this better…I
feel responsible because…."

"Why is this any of your business, Mrs. Ross?" she interrupted again. "Surely the police know what they're doing."

"Please let me try to explain," I blurted out.

She stopped interrupting me, waiting now to hear my
explanation. Her eyes had narrowed, clearly viewing me with
suspicion.

"Okay," I said. "You already know I told the police about
Jack Hines. Well, his mother called me a little while ago. She

accused me of implicating him, and...well, she made me feel guilty about the whole thing. She claims he's innocent."

Rella Cox was still looking at me with suspicion. But her face had changed. Anger was rippling beneath the stony surface.

Suddenly she erupted. "Jack Hines! I told Kay not to hire that man! I told her you don't hire a man like that to work at a nursery school."

"You tried to stop her from hiring him?"

"Of course I did! But what was my opinion worth? Not much! Kay was happy to let me do all the dull routine work around here, but when it came right down to it, she made all the decisions. Jack Hines was nothing compared to some of the other things going on around here."

"Like what?"

"Like Kidd's Korner!" she spat out. She seemed to regret her words as soon as they left her mouth.

"Kidd's Korner?" I asked, trying to look ingenuous. "What's that?"

She took a deep breath and clenched her teeth. She was holding a lot back. Finally she let go. "Kidd's Korner is a chain of day-care centers run by a man named Gabriel Kidd. He's branching out in this part of the country, and for some reason he focused his attention on East Winnette. I have no idea why." She shook her head in disbelief. "A few months ago, Kay told me she was considering selling this school to Kidd. Apparently he offered her a fantastic amount for it, and she thought she'd be crazy not to sell. I told her it was a rotten idea, but she wouldn't listen."

"Why was it such a bad idea?"

"To begin with, I don't think a national chain belongs here. We have a tradition of independence on the North Shore.

Why, you can hardly find a fast-food franchise around here!" I thought of the McDonald's in Kenilwood and silently thanked Providence that at least one franchise had snuck in.

"Did anything else bother you?"

"Well...yes!" Her face was filled with rage, and she seemed eager now to vent her spleen. "I've put twelve years of my life into this school, and I had every right to expect that I'd take over as director someday. Kay was thinking of retiring in the next few years, you know. She planned to stay on as owner—she and her husband owned the school—but she was going to give up the directorship and maybe give up teaching as well. From everything she said, I was led to believe that I'd take over as director when she retired. But along comes Gabriel Kidd with a pot full of money, and I get left out in the cold. Some reward for all the time and hard work I put into this place!"

"Did you really think you would have been treated like that?"

"Well, no, I didn't know that for sure," she said. "But I did some research into Kidd's Korner. Gabriel Kidd apparently has no compunctions about firing all the employees at the schools he buys and putting in his own staff. That way he can be sure they'll be loyal to him, I suppose, and not have any ideas of their own."

Rella Cox began shaking her head again. "What is this world coming to, when we have one man running nursery schools all over this country? It makes me sick...."

She turned away and looked out her window. The sunny, crisp weather had changed to a pervasive gray gloom, and dry autumn leaves swirled outside the window.

I interrupted her reverie. "Now that Mrs. Boyer's dead, what will happen to the nursery school?"

Rella Cox turned back to face me. "I hardly know what to say. I suppose the board will meet to discuss it. Kay's husband is now the sole owner, of course, and he'll make the ultimate decision. But he's never taken any interest in the school. The board may be able to influence him, maybe even convince him not to sell.

"The bottom line is I don't know what the outcome will be. But in the meantime, I've assumed the role of acting director." A barely noticeable smile crept across her face. She had triumphed after all, for the moment at least.

"Do you think you'll be asked to stay on as director?"

"If Tom Boyer decides against selling to Kidd's Korner, I'd say that's likely," she said. "But it remains to be seen, Mrs. Ross, it remains to be seen. I can't tell you any more than that." She glanced at the clock on the wall of her office. "And now I'm afraid I have to ask you to leave. I have another appointment in a few minutes."

"Please, I just have another question or two. About Jack Hines," I said.

"Very well. Ask away." The smile had vanished again. I knew her patience was wearing thin, and I had to ask my questions fast.

"Did he turn out to be a good worker?" I asked. "I know you were opposed to hiring him, but did he do a good job once he started?"

"If you call stealing doing a good job, then he did a good job," she snorted.

"Stealing?"

"Yes, stealing. I think he got into the petty cash, but Kay said she couldn't prove it. She said it might have been one of the mothers who took the money. As if the mothers in East Winnette need to steal from petty cash! I told Kay to report it to the police, but she refused. She said it didn't amount to much, that he deserved another chance."

"How did he get along with Kay?"

Ms. Cox paused to think about it. "They seemed to get along all right. I don't think they had much interaction. He was just a janitor here, you know."

"Do you think he disliked Kay for some reason...enough to want to harm her?"

"I really couldn't say. But if they had a run-in of some kind, it's possible. A man like that is capable of anything."

"But if he didn't....is there anyone else who might have had problems with her...?"

Ms. Cox looked away from me and thought for a moment before turning back to face me. "Mrs. Thurgood...have you met Mrs. Thurgood?"

I nodded.

"She used to teach here a number of years ago. Just before I came here. I think Kay and Betty Thurgood had some sort of dreadful argument back then. It led to Betty's quitting and going to work in Glenview Park. There was bad blood between the two of them ever since.

"Then there's Kay's family, of course. Kay was all sweetness and light here at school, but the truth is her family life was a terrible mess."

"It was?" Kay Boyer had a messed-up family life? The idea was patently ridiculous. A woman of such patience, such devotion to children...how could her own family be less than perfect? She'd treated our daughters with infinite care. That time we had to take Missy to the ER after she fell in the playground and twisted her ankle–Kay Boyer couldn't do enough to make sure that Missy was handled carefully and cautiously.

"I can see you don't believe me," Rella Cox interrupted. "Why don't you meet her family and see for yourself? The funeral's tomorrow, and you'll have a perfect excuse to talk to them if you go."

Great idea. "Thanks, Ms. Cox. You've been an enormous help. I'm sorry I took so much of your time," I said. I got up and shook her hand. It felt icy.

"I was happy to help," she said unconvincingly. "Let me know what you find out."

Trying to digest all the new information stuffed into my head, I got into the Toyota and drove home. But between a phone call from my aunt, a skinned knee Missy brought home, a crisis when Tammy's other ear fell off, and take-out Chinese food for dinner, Kay Boyer's murder slipped out of my consciousness for a few blessed hours. I even slept well that night, waking only once to wonder who the hell Joshua was and why Rella Cox had anointed him as artist-of-the-month.

CHAPTER 12

Friday morning I got up early and raced outside to grab the *Tribune*, hoping no one would see me in my nightgown.

The air was misty again, and the paper felt damp. Once inside, I turned to the obituaries. There it was: Katherine Boyer, age 53, funeral at 10:00 a.m. at the Royce Funeral Home on 9th Street in East Winnette. I tore the notice out of the paper and stuck it in my purse.

The time of the funeral presented a problem. Lindsay didn't leave for school till 12:30, and Marv had a ten o'clock class again. I'd have to ask a neighbor to watch Lindsay.

The house was still quiet. I made a pot of coffee and some toast and glanced quickly through the rest of the paper. One of the ads caught my eye. Kroch's, our favorite bookstore in nearby Evanston, was holding a book-signing that afternoon. Gabriel Kidd, successful entrepreneur, would be signing copies of his new book, *Little Things Mean a Lot: The Gabriel Kidd Story*, at one o'clock.

I couldn't believe my luck. Gabriel Kidd was on a book tour. And amazingly, he'd be appearing at a bookstore just one or two suburbs away.

The man's timing couldn't have been better. I tore out the ad and stuck it in my purse next to Kay Boyer's obit.

Everyone else was soon downstairs, and I got busy helping Marv and Missy get off to school. Once they were gone, and Lindsay was deciding which Snoopy t-shirt to wear to school, I called my neighbor, Darlene Dawson. Darlene's kids were the same ages as mine, and Matthew was in Lindsay's class at the nursery school.

"Hello." I recognized Darlene's nasal voice.

"Hi, Darlene. It's Alison Ross."

"Oh, hi, Alison! I've been meaning to call you. I hear you found Mrs. Boyer's body. *What happened?*" Darlene's appetite for neighborhood gossip was insatiable.

"It's a long story, Darlene. I'll tell you all about it another time, but right now I'd like to ask a favor of you."

"Oh." Darlene sounded disappointed. "What is it?"

"Could Lindsay could come over to play with Matthew and stay for lunch at your house today? An emergency has come up." I tried to sound desperate. In a way, I was.

"Well, I guess so. I wasn't planning to go anywhere till I took Matthew to school," Darlene said. "What happened?"

"There's been a death in my family," I lied. "The funeral's this morning, and I couldn't get a babysitter."

"I know how that is," Darlene commiserated. "Lord, do I ever. Sure, bring Lindsay over anytime. We'll be here."

"Thanks, Darlene. We'll be over right away."

Lindsay and I got dressed in record time and dashed down the block to Darlene's. Darlene met us at the door, and Lindsay zoomed inside to look for Matthew.

"Do you want to come in for a minute?" Darlene asked. She was still in her bathrobe, the thick terrycloth kind they sold at the Lands' End outlet in downtown Evanston. I snuck a quick look at the monogram on the pocket: RMG. A Lands' End reject, all right.

"Thanks, no," I said. "I don't have time right now."

"Funny. I was just reading the paper, and Mrs. Boyer's funeral is this morning, too. A coincidence, huh?"

"Yeah, it really is," I nodded, feeling uncomfortable. I wasn't used to lying, and I usually botched it.

"If I'd read the paper earlier, I might have asked you to watch Matthew so I could go to her funeral," Darlene said. Had she guessed the truth? "But what the heck, it's not that important. Not like family." There was no hint of sarcasm in her voice. Maybe she'd bought my story after all.

"Well, thanks a million, Darlene," I said, turning to leave. "I'll take care of Matthew for you sometime." I hoped she wouldn't try to cash in on that promise anytime soon. Matthew was a monster.

I ran down her steps and back to my house, where I jumped into the Toyota. I'd never been to the Royce Funeral Home, but I knew it was located six blocks past the nursery school.

Kay Boyer clearly hadn't traveled very far since Tuesday morning. I felt vaguely sick to my stomach as I parked the Toyota in the spacious Royce lot.

It was nearly ten o'clock when I walked through the doors of the Georgian red-brick building. "Mrs. Boyer?" a man in a black suit inquired. I nodded. "First room on the left."

The room was already crowded. I took one of the few remaining seats in a back row. With my vantage point behind almost everyone else, I recognized a lot of heads of hair from the nursery school, mostly those of mothers who were on the board. Mary Beth Bannister's frizzy brown mop stood out a mile among the other mothers' smooth blond locks.

I noticed Andrea Lewis, sitting near the front in an elegant black suit. Her hair was perfectly coiffed, as always. I didn't see Rella Cox anywhere.

I craned my neck but couldn't make out the faces of any of the family members in the front row. I didn't see a casket either.

The service began on time and was mercifully brief. The minister dwelled upon Kay Boyer's devotion to her school but said surprisingly little about her family, just a few words about her "dear husband and children." And although he made no direct reference to Kay's having been murdered, he spoke of the "senseless tragedy of a vibrant woman struck down in the very prime of her life."

A nice multi-purpose phrase, suitable for your basic run-of-the-mill tragedy, mouthed by just about every member of the clergy who presides at one of these events.

At the end of the service, the minister mentioned that the family would receive visitors at their home at 2200 Magnolia Street immediately after the service. Nothing about a burial or a trip to the cemetery. Either Kay was being cremated, or the police hadn't yet authorized her burial.

I pulled out the obituary notice I'd stuck in my purse and glanced at the names of the survivors: husband Thomas, son Wesley, daughter Bree, granddaughter Emily. Suddenly I didn't want to meet any of them. Maybe I'd go straight home.

Walking to the parking lot, I reconsidered. What did I have to lose? If I felt uncomfortable at the Boyer house, I could always mumble some sympathetic words and leave. I decided to drive to 2200 Magnolia and see how I felt when I got there.

The house sat on a small corner lot in a less-affluent part of East Winnette. It was an old white frame house, and it had clearly been neglected in recent years. The paint on the exterior walls was peeling, and the concrete front steps had began to crumble.

I sat in the Toyota for a few minutes to give the family a chance to get home and prepare for the onslaught of visitors. While I waited, I took another look at the names listed in the obituary. Thomas, Wesley, Bree, Emily.

A moment later I noticed another car pull up, and I figured I should probably go in. As one of the first visitors, I could talk to the family before a lot of people arrived. Then, if things got awkward, I could leave early. I carefully made my way up the crumbling steps and rang the doorbell.

The door opened a crack, and a little girl about Missy's age peered out at me. Six years old or thereabouts. She had long brown hair and a solemn look on her face. "You must be Emily," I said. "May I come in?"

Emily didn't say anything but opened the door all the way. I walked past her into a large dimly-lit living room. A young woman was hurrying about the room, turning on some lamps and putting ashtrays on the tables. She was tall and slim, with a cap of curly brown hair, and appeared to be in her early 20s. "Hello," she said, looking puzzled. I knew she was wondering who I was.

"My name's Alison Ross. I knew Mrs. Boyer at the nursery school."

"Oh, yes, Mrs. Ross. Your name sounds familiar," she said, nodding her head. "I'm Bree Boyer." She walked closer to me and shook my hand. Her grip was firmer than I expected.

"I'm so very sorry, Ms. Boyer," I said, looking into her eyes. They were a deep blue and very sad.

"Thank you. Please call me Bree." She walked over to a worn-looking sofa and offered me a seat next to her.

"Please call me Alison," I said. I really didn't know what else to say.

"Did you know my mother well?" she asked, trying to make small talk. I looked around the room. Emily had gone over to sit in the lap of a young man who looked several years older than Bree. Was that Wesley Boyer? Was Emily his child?

"No, not very well," I said. "But I was at the nursery school Tuesday morning, and I...I...."

"And you found my mother's body," she finished. "Now I remember where I heard your name."

I nodded.

"And you saw Jack Hines leaving the room, didn't you?" she asked. I nodded again. "It was lucky you saw him, or the police might never have found the killer," she said pensively. "I guess we should all be grateful you were there." A hint of irony crept into her voice.

"That's true," I said. "Assuming Jack Hines *is* the killer."

She looked startled. "What?" We stared at each other. "You mean you don't think he is?"

"I'm not sure. He says he's innocent."

"Well, why would you believe anything a man like that says?" she asked. "He's got a criminal record a mile long. And he's certainly not going to admit he did it if he thinks he's got a chance of getting off."

"That's true," I agreed. "But it still bothers me. The evidence against him is purely circumstantial, and I'd feel a lot better about it if I thought no one else could have possibly done it."

"Well...well, that's understandable, I suppose." Her face looked troubled. The certainty she'd had, that Jack Hines was the killer, was suddenly in doubt. The doorbell rang, and Bree rose to answer it. Just then I saw a gray-haired man, stooped and painfully thin, enter the room from somewhere in the back of the house.

He seated himself in a chair in a dark corner of the room and began shaking his head and mumbling to himself. No one else in the room appeared to notice. Bree, the young man, and

Emily were preoccupied with the new visitors. I crossed the room and sat down next to the older man.

"Excuse me, sir. I'm Alison Ross."

He looked up, surprised at the interruption. He struggled to regain his composure, then stuck out a gnarled, brown-spotted hand. "Tom Boyer, Miss Ross. Did you know my wife?"

I was shocked to learn that this debilitated man was Mrs. Boyer's husband. Bob Shakespear had said her husband was "much older," but I hadn't imagined that he was a good twenty years older than Kay. And apparently not in very good health.

"Yes, Mr. Boyer, I did. She was a wonderful woman."

"Yes, yes, she was," he said. "I...I just can't believe she's gone." His head began to shake again. He seemed to be truly in despair, desolate without his wife.

I tried some consoling words. "Well, at least you know you had a happy life together, all these years. That's something to be grateful for."

"Happy?" He paused for a moment. "Oh, yes, we had some happy times. But we had some pretty rough times, too, you know. Julie...." His voice drifted off.

"Julie?" It was obviously a name I should have known but didn't.

"Our older daughter. A beautiful girl," Tom said. His despair seemed to have deepened. He looked into my eyes. "You remember about Julie, don't you?"

"No, Mr. Boyer. I'm sorry, I don't." What had happened to Julie? Her name hadn't appeared in Kay's obituary.

He seemed unable to speak. Instead, he began wringing his hands. I couldn't help noticing the plethora of ugly brown spots that covered them. I silently resolved to wear white gloves every summer for the rest of my life.

Finally he spoke again. "Our Julie...our Julie took...took her own life." He had difficulty getting the words out. I was pretty startled to hear them.

"Ten years ago, a few weeks before Christmas. God almighty, what a Christmas present Kay and I got that year! Our darling Julie gone. And now Kay. I don't think I can go on...."

"But you must," I said quickly.

Why did I say that? I didn't even know this man. But consoling people is apparently in my DNA. I always try to console, to make other people feel better. An analyst would probably say I have a deep-seated need to be loved that manifests itself in this kind of behavior.

"You have so much to live for," I continued. "Look at the rest of your family. You have another lovely daughter, and a son, and a granddaughter. They need you now, more than ever."

The old man's face seemed to brighten for a moment. "Yes, yes, I suppose so. Bree...my Bree's doing all right at that business college she goes to. She's got a part-time job there, too. And my son....my son Wes has turned out pretty well. He was a problem kid, you know, but he straightened out, he even got married and had his little girl. But Wes...." Tom's face changed, the brightness gone. "His marriage busted up a couple of years ago, and that record store of his...it's not doing too well."

"Wes has a record store?"

Tom Boyer nodded his head. "That little one in West Winnette, over on Hardy Boulevard. I don't think he's making a living there. But he never tells me anything anymore."

"A lot of men have trouble communicating that way," I said, hoping my pop psychology would make him feel better.

This man had had a rotten life, that was for sure. One calamity after another. He began coughing, a deep-chested smoker's cough. The coughing turned into sobs, and I decided to leave.

"Excuse me, Mr. Boyer, I have to be leaving," I said.

He gained some control over his sobs and looked up at me. "Sure, sure, go ahead, young lady. Thank you for coming by." He shook my hand again.

I turned and looked for the front door. Bree was greeting a new guest. Another mother from the nursery school.

"Goodbye, Bree," I said, waving in her direction.

"Oh, goodbye now, Alison. Thank you for coming."

I ran down the stairs outside, nearly tripping on the broken concrete. I couldn't wait to escape from that depressing old house.

CHAPTER 13

I got home about noon, heated a can of soup for lunch, and began to leaf through the *Tribune* again. Halfway through, I saw the hole where the bookstore ad had been. Gabriel Kidd! I'd forgotten all about him.

I gulped down my soup and flew out the door, headed for downtown Evanston. Parking near Kroch's was a bitch, and I wondered if I'd be able to stash the Toyota in time to see Gabriel Kidd.

Luckily, a parking spot just down the block from Kroch's opened up as I approached. I zoomed in and tossed a few coins in the parking meter. By one o'clock, I was inside Kroch's, where employees were busily setting up a table for the book-signing.

Suddenly I heard a commotion in the rear of the store. I turned and recognized the store manager. He was entering with a tall, rugged-looking man sporting a deep tan and a thick mane of white hair. The white-haired man strode through the store with confidence, sporting an almost regal bearing.

It was clearly Gabriel Kidd. A small crowd immediately gathered around him.

"Please line up, everyone. You'll all get a chance to talk to Mr. Kidd," the manager said. "Remember, you must purchase Mr. Kidd's book before you get in line if you want him to sign it."

Several people were already clutching copies of the book. A few others broke away from the crowd and walked over to the display to get one. I paused, uncertain whether I wanted to buy it.

I made my way to the display and picked up a copy. I figured I could always give it to someone as a gift. Besides, I couldn't see another way to get close to Gabriel Kidd.

I shelled out my $12.95 plus tax, and got in line. At least a dozen people were ahead of me, and it looked like a long wait. I read the dust jacket, then began skimming the book itself.

Kidd appeared to be a genuine rags-to-riches success story. After a childhood spent in the shadow of the Pittsburgh steel mills, he'd raised capital for a series of successful business ventures. Finally, in the mid-'70s, noting the increasing demand for quality child-care, he'd come up with the concept of a nationwide chain of day-care centers. I couldn't help wondering whether his interest in small children had been influenced in any way by his having the name Kidd.

Influenced or not, he'd entered the market by buying up a large number of existing nursery schools, first in California, then elsewhere in the country, imposing his own ideas of child care on what were formerly independently run schools. The book's description of his methods made him out to be a benevolent man primarily concerned with children's needs, but between the lines appeared a hard-driving entrepreneur who'd seen a social vacuum and filled it.

I was finally near the head of the line, close enough to observe Gabriel Kidd interacting with other customers. He was oozing charm and self-confidence, making small talk with every one of them as they approached the table.

The fiftyish woman in front of me handed her book to Kidd with a tremulous smile. She seemed slightly agog to be meeting even a low-grade celebrity. "Mr. Kidd, it's such a pleasure to meet you," she was saying. "I'm a nursery school teacher, and I took the afternoon off so I could meet you. They think I'm sick," she added with a nervous laugh.

"Well, I'm flattered," Kidd answered, smiling. "But I hope they can spare you. Those children need a good teacher like you." The man's charm was limitless.

"Oh, yes, don't worry," the woman said.

"What name shall I put here?" Kidd asked.

"Shirley...Shirley Armstrong," she answered. "You know, Mr. Kidd, they were saying at my school that you were interested in buying it. Is that true?"

"Which school is that, Shirley?" Kidd finished signing the book and looked up at her.

"North Evanston Nursery School."

"North Evanston...North Evanston.... That does ring a bell, but I can't remember exactly.... Please forgive me," he said, flashing another dazzling smile.

"Oh, that's okay," she said. She glanced over at me and the others in line behind me. "Well, I guess I have to go now. Thanks for signing my book."

"My pleasure." Kidd gave her one last smile, then looked over at me expectantly.

"And what name shall I write in this book, young lady?" he asked.

"Umm...just sign your name. That'll be fine."

"Is it a gift?"

"Yes, that's right," I said. "It's a gift."

"I can make it out to whomever you say, you know," he offered.

"No, that's all right. I'm not sure who I'm giving it to." A sudden inspiration hit. "I was planning to give it to Kay Boyer, but...."

His head jerked up sharply. "Did you say Kay Boyer?"

"Yes. She was the director of my daughter's nursery school, but now she's...she's dead."

Kidd was silent. He looked away from me for a moment. "I knew Kay Boyer," he finally said, looking back at me. He had large hazel eyes, framed by massive white eyebrows. Could those be tears welling up in them? "I just heard that she died," he added. "Tragic. Such an attractive, vital woman."

"Yes, she was," I agreed. "Did you know she was murdered?" I watched his face carefully when I said it.

"Yes, I did." He appeared unsurprised. "My secretary saw an item in one of the Chicago newspapers and told me about it. I was shocked, really shocked. We were about to close a deal, you know. I was quite excited about moving into East Winnette. But now...now I'm not sure where I stand. I may have to look at some other schools on the North Shore."

The man behind me began to cough, the kind of cough people fake to get attention. I glanced at him. He looked annoyed and pointed to his watch. "Some people have other things to do today, miss," he said.

"Sorry," I said. I turned back to Gabriel Kidd. "I have to go now...."

"Let me give you my phone number," he said quickly. He produced a business card, turned it over, and wrote a number on it. "That's my room at the Ritz-Carlton. Give me a call tonight. I'd like to talk to you about Kay."

Robotically, I extended my hand and took the card. "Thanks, I will," I said. I turned and walked out of Kroch's, clutching Kidd's business card. I wasn't sure why he'd given it to me or why he had any desire to talk to me again.

CHAPTER 14

I walked through my back door, exhausted. First the funeral, then the Boyer home, then Gabriel Kidd. I felt like collapsing. But it was 2:15, and the girls would be coming home at 3. I had to call Bob Shakespear now.

I poured a Diet Pepsi, called the police station, and asked to speak to him.

A moment later he answered.

"It's Alison Ross."

"Oh, Mrs. Ross. How's it going?"

"You can call me Alison."

"Fine. Call me Bob. Now what can I do for you?"

"I got a call from Jack Hines's mother yesterday. She says he didn't do it."

"What? She called you? Good God," he said. "Did it upset you?"

"Yes," I admitted.

"Jeez, now felons' mothers are harassing our witnesses. I've gotta do something about it," he said.

"Wait a minute, Bob. I feel sorry for the poor woman. She *is* his mother. Besides," I added, "he's not really a felon. He hasn't been proven guilty yet."

"Sorry, Alison," he said, laughing. "Now I remember, you're a lawyer. I'll have to watch what I say around you. By the way, are you in practice anywhere?"

"Not at the moment," I said. I didn't feel like launching into a discussion of my aborted career just then, so before he could say anything else, I resumed talking. "Listen, Bob, I've been thinking about everything. Are you still sure Jack Hines did it? I mean, can you prove his knife is the murder weapon?"

"The knife...the knife is something of a problem, I'll be honest with you. We're still not certain what size or shape of knife was involved. But we're working on it. And I have no problem with Hines as the killer. He was there, he had a motive, and he had a knife on him when we arrested him. Besides," he asked, "who else would have wanted to kill her?"

"Have you determined exactly where Mrs. Boyer was when she was stabbed?"

"Apparently she was standing near the chest where you found her," he said. "Hines must have stabbed her, she fell into the chest, and he covered her up with some of those old clothes. We couldn't find her blood anyplace else in the room, and no evidence that her body was brought in from outside."

"Did you find any of her blood on Jack Hines's things?"

"No, we didn't," he admitted. "But he could have dumped the clothes he was wearing when he killed her. We're looking for them right now. And the knife–he could have washed off the knife, of course."

"Of course," I said. "What time was she killed?"

"The medical examiner says it was about 8 or 8:30 that morning," he said. "She generally got to school early and set things up before anyone else got there. So her getting there by 8 wasn't unusual."

"Do you know anything about a suicide in Kay Boyer's family?"

"You mean her daughter?" he asked. "Yeah, I know about it. The older one, Julie, was a suicide about ten years ago. It was one of those teen-age suicides nobody can explain. She was 18, doing pretty well in school, had a bunch of friends, but one day she came home from school and hanged herself."

I shuddered. "How awful. I wonder how her parents lived through it."

"These teen suicides aren't that unusual on the North Shore," Bob said. "The kids are under a lot of pressure. They may have money, but money doesn't buy happiness, you know."

"Really?" I tried to sound sarcastic. He didn't notice.

"You know how it happens," he went on. "The parents are busy and don't have much time for the kids, but they expect them to do well at everything anyway. Sometimes the kids just can't cope."

That wasn't going to happen to my kids. Not if I could help it. "Was their son in trouble, too, at one point?"

"Their son...their son.... Let me think...." I imagined his round face deep in thought, even wrinkling a bit around the eyes. "Oh, yeah, that's Wes Boyer, the one who owns the record store. I checked him out. You're right, he was a troublemaker in high school. Set a fire in the school auditorium. Trying to get attention from his parents, I guess. A lot of kids around here do that kind of thing, too. But he straightened out after that and quit making trouble."

The revelations were whirling around in my head. "Listen, Bob, you've been great. Thanks for your time." I said goodbye and hung up.

Quarter to three. I had to get over to the nursery school in a few minutes. But first I had just enough time to take a quick look at the pile of mail sitting on our front porch.

I sat down in the dining room and began sorting through the pile. There were pleas for money from what appeared to be an inordinate number of the charitable institutions in North

America. I immediately threw out most of them. The others made me feel guilty, sufficiently guilty that I put them in a haphazard stack on the dining room sideboard, to be dealt with at a later time.

I also found a couple of bills, a letter from my college roommate, the Harvard Law School alumni bulletin, and a small smudged envelope with an unfamiliar return address. The handwriting on the envelope was a florid one I'd never seen before.

I opened the smudged envelope and pulled out two crisp twenty-dollar bills. A note, written on a plain white piece of paper, was clipped to the bills. It read:

> Enclosed please find $40. Please help me
> prove my son is innocint.
> Yours very truly,
> Elmira Hines

CHAPTER 15

I stuffed the note and money from Elmira Hines back inside the smudged envelope and stuck it in a drawer in the dining room sideboard. The drawer where I stash cash and important papers I don't want sticky little fingers to touch. Then I dashed over to the nursery school to pick up Lindsay.

Today was a day I wouldn't have minded being in a carpool—if someone else were driving, that is.

I'd tried a carpool one year with Missy, but it proved to be more frustrating than it was worth. I always seemed to live closer to the school than the other mothers in the carpool, and I wound up driving twice as far as anybody else.

But the worst part was stuffing Missy into her multiple layers of clothes every winter (underwear, shirt, pants, sweater, snowsuit, hat, muffler, mittens, boots) and then waiting for her carpool pick-up. Sometimes we waited and waited, while her body temperature elevated to an astronomical level.

One time a mother forgot to pick her up at all. Missy was decked out in her new pink snowsuit and at least three woolly, sweaty layers underneath. Looking like a plump pink bird, she waited by the living room window for twenty minutes before we realized that the carpool had come and gone without her. After that, I said goodbye to carpools and relied exclusively on Marv and me to get our kids where they had to go.

By 3:20, Lindsay was busily attacking a Minnie Mouse coloring book along with a snack of apples and peanut butter, but Missy wasn't home yet. I glanced out the living room window, but I didn't see her. She should have been home by now. Where was she?

I left Lindsay alone for a minute while I ran down the front steps and looked all the way down the block, to the corner where she turned on her way home from school. No Missy.

I felt panic rising inside me. Where was she? I began to imagine scenarios too horrific to imagine. I'd seen a gardener raking leaves at a home on the next block when I drove by on the way back from the nursery school. He could have grabbed my darling little Missy as she walked by.

There were stories like that on the Chicago TV news broadcasts all the time. Nothing like that had ever happened in East Winnette, but....there was always a first time.

Now I couldn't help berating myself. I usually tried to pick up Missy on my way back from the nursery school. *Why didn't I pick her up today?* Okay, I'd barely made it to the nursery school on time, and I'd rushed back with Lindsay, expecting Missy to walk home with the other kids.

But I should have picked her up!

I ran back into the house to check on Lindsay. She was coloring Minnie Mouse without a care in the world. *But where was Missy?*

My heart was pounding, and suddenly a chilling thought hit me. Could this be the result of my probing into Kay Boyer's murder? That possibility was too horrible to consider.

I ran down the front steps again and nearly collapsed in relief. Missy was coming down the block, stumbling as she walked, carrying one shoe. I ran towards her and gave her an enormous hug.

"What happened, sweetheart?" I said. "You're late."

"I know. I'm sorry, Mommy." Her small face looked troubled.

"Where's your other shoe?"

"I lost it," she said. "I looked everywhere for it. Are you mad at me?"

"No, no, of course not. But how could you lose one shoe?" Missy started to cry, and I decided to stop asking questions and give her another hug. She was clearly upset that she'd lost one of her shiny new leather shoes, purchased when school began in September, but all I cared about was having her in my arms, safe and sound.

Once Missy was inside and busy with a math workbook, I tried to relax, take a deep breath, and get my nervous system back to normal. Finally I had a moment to think about the envelope from Elmira Hines.

Why had she sent it? Did she think she could win me over to her cause with forty dollars? Surely she realized that people in East Winnette, even those at the lower end of the socioeconomic scale (like college professors and unemployed lawyers), wouldn't be influenced by such a paltry amount.

Did she actually intend to hire me? To help her prove that her son was innocent? She *had* sounded desperate on the phone. Desperate, and convinced of his innocence. And equally convinced that I could help her prove it.

But could I? The halfhearted attempts I'd made so far hadn't gotten me anywhere. All this business about the nursery school being sold, and the suicide in Kay Boyer's family—that didn't prove anything. Of course, I still didn't know very much about Kay Boyer, and I knew even less about Jack Hines.

Maybe if I made a few more phone calls. Maybe if I talked to a few more people....

Wait a minute, Alison. What are you getting yourself into? You're no detective, remember? You're just a stay-at-home mom right now. You don't even work in the profession you've trained for and practiced, remember? And now you want to suddenly be a detective?

I poured myself a Diet Pepsi and carried it outside to our front porch. I sat down on a wicker chair, part of the summer furniture we hadn't gotten around to putting away. We usually waited until the first snow, prolonging the illusion that Chicago really had six months of weather suitable for sitting on front porches.

The fresh air seemed to clear my mind. Why not keep Elmira Hines's money? I could talk to a few more people, and if I found I was going nowhere, I could always return it. But if I thought I was making progress, learning things the police had missed, then I could keep the money as payment for my work.

Wasn't I always talking about getting a part-time job? Now one had fallen into my lap. How could I turn it down?

I was curious about the murder anyway. After all, I *had* found Kay Boyer's body. I couldn't walk away from the murder even if I wanted to. So why not investigate it? And if I was now a working detective on a retainer (albeit a pathetic one), so much the better.

I suddenly remembered Jimmy Stewart in "Call Northside 777," an old B movie that's set in Chicago. I'd seen it on late-night TV at least twice. The mother of a convicted murderer convinces newspaper-reporter Jimmy that her son is innocent, and he sets out to prove it.

Ta-dah! Jimmy Stewart would no longer have to struggle alone. I, Alison Ross, seeker of truth, had joined him in the noble fight against wrongdoing in the American criminal justice system.

I decided not to tell Marv about Elmira Hines just yet. I had to decide exactly what and how to tell him. If he thought I was doing something dangerous, he would certainly object.

But there was something I couldn't put off any longer: I had to talk to Jack Hines. I dreaded having to call him to get his side of the story. But I couldn't ignore him anymore, not if I was going to take his mother's money.

Getting in touch with him at Cook County Jail was harder than I thought it would be. When I tried reaching him Friday night, after a slap-dash dinner of canned corn and Cheese-to-Please pizza (our local favorite), I had to call a dozen times before someone at the jail picked up the phone.

Finally someone answered. "Who's calling?" a gruff voice asked.

"This is one of his lawyers," I improvised. "I need to speak to him right away."

"I'll have to take your name and number, miss. He'll call you back."

"Tell him it's important." I gave my name and number to the voice and hung up.

Getting through to Gabriel Kidd was a lot easier. I phoned his room at the Ritz-Carlton about eleven o'clock, after Marv had gone to bed. The phone rang only once.

"Yes?" he answered.

"Mr. Kidd? This is Alison Ross. We met at the bookstore in Evanston this afternoon. You gave me this number."

"What?" He sounded surprised by the call. "The bookstore?"

"I hope I'm not disturbing you," I said quickly. "I know it's kind of late to call, but I figured you'd be out for dinner and...."

"No, no, I'm always up till one or two in the morning," he assured me. "I've never been the type who needs a lot of sleep. Please tell me exactly why you're calling"

Now I was the one who was surprised. "Well, you suggested that I call you. You gave me this number on one of your business cards."

He didn't answer. He'd obviously forgotten meeting me.

"I mentioned Kay Boyer, and you...."

"Kay Boyer! Oh, yes, you're the woman who knew Kay Boyer. Now I remember," he said. "I wanted to ask you about Kay's murder. I heard about it from my secretary, who saw the obituary in a copy of the *Tribune*, or maybe it was the *Sun-Times*. But I'd like to hear a first-hand report of just what happened."

"Well, it's not exactly clear," I said. "She was apparently murdered at the nursery school early Tuesday morning. She was stabbed. I found her body there a short time later...."

"You found her body?"

"Yes. Yes, I did. I guess that's why I've gotten involved," I blurted out.

"Involved? Involved in what?"

"I'm trying to find out what happened. Because I found her body." I didn't mention Elmira Hines.

"I'm pretty shook up about this myself. Kay and I had become rather close during the past few months. We met several times, and we hit it off pretty well. She was planning to retire as director of the nursery school soon anyway, and when I offered her a good price for it, she was ecstatic. She clearly needed the money. Her husband's not well, and her kids were somewhat dependent on her financially. Besides, the nursery school wasn't bringing in a lot of money."

"I see." I'd never thought of the nursery school as a major money-maker. I didn't think it was supposed to be. "But tell me, how do you make these schools so profitable?"

What *did* Kidd do to turn a bunch of penny-ante nursery schools into a lucrative multimillion-dollar operation?

"Well, once I take over, the schools become totally different entities. First, I turn them into full-time day-care centers. Parents who want quality day-care are willing to pay many times what parents pay for a traditional nursery school. Second, I institute economies of scale, which I can do because I operate nationwide. I buy equipment and supplies in volume, and so forth."

This sounded like a spiel Kidd might have given to a chamber of commerce somewhere. It probably was.

"Forgive me for changing the subject," I said, "but....do you know why anyone might have wanted to kill Kay Boyer? You met with her recently, and you seem to know a lot about her family and what was happening at the school."

He paused. "No...not really. I know Kay was troubled. Her life didn't seem to be going very well, and she seemed anxious to change her situation. I think she saw my purchase of the school as a solution to some of her difficulties. But I also know she had some pretty stiff opposition from that assistant of hers."

"Rella Cox?"

"Yes, I think that's the name," he said. "Kay told me that woman was dead-set against my purchase of the school."

"Can you think of anything else?"

"Well, her family...certainly her family presented problems for her. I'm afraid I don't know any details. Does any of this add up to murder?"

"I don't know."

"Nor do I. But this janitor they arrested–he sounds like a logical suspect. Why don't you just leave things to the police? They generally know what they're doing."

Generally, yes. But maybe not this time.

"Well, thanks a lot, Mr. Kidd," I said. You've been very helpful."

"Certainly, uh....what did you say your name was?"

"Alison. Alison Ross."

"Right. Listen, Alison, you have my business card. Anything comes up, feel free to call me at that number. You can call collect. I'd be happy to talk to you anytime."

"Thanks, Mr. Kidd. I'll remember that."

Gabriel Kidd said goodbye, and I headed straight for bed.

CHAPTER 16

I was dreaming of a tall white-haired man, confidently taking me into his arms, when I sensed something stirring the air around me. I slowly opened my eyes and saw Lindsay standing next to my bed. "Hi, Mommy!" she said. "What are we going to do today?"

"Oh, I don't know, honey. We'll see." I was tired and felt like going back to sleep, but that was impossible now. I looked over at Marv. Still sleeping. I never understood why Lindsay always woke me up but didn't wake him.

"Get up, Mommy, get up! I'm hungry," Lindsay said. "Missy is, too."

"Where's Missy?"

"Watching cartoons." Of course. It was Saturday morning, and the usual festival of wretched cartoons would be blasting away on the TV downstairs. I dragged myself out of bed and down the stairs, preparing to face the Bugs Bunny Hour one more time.

After breakfast with the girls, I decided to get dressed and drop in on Wes Boyer's record store. Missy and Lindsay begged to go along. They were even willing to miss some of their favorite cartoons just so they could be with Mommy. That made me feel pretty good, even if it did cramp my style.

"Okay, okay," I finally agreed. The girls ran upstairs to get dressed, and I followed them to look in on Marv. Still sleeping.

The three of us drove to Hardy Boulevard in West Winnette. I'd never noticed a record store, but the busy street had two or three charmless strip malls, and I figured the record store had to be in one of them. We found it in the second one we tried.

"In Record Time" read a small hand-painted sign in the window. He really must be hurting for cash, I thought; he can't even pay for a decent sign. I parked the Toyota, and the girls and I entered the store.

"You two can look through the children's records," I said. "If you find something good, I might buy it for you." The girls ran off, looking for the children's section.

They didn't have far to go. The store was small and didn't appear to be well-stocked.

I made my way to the classical section, looking around for Wes Boyer as I went. There was no sign of him, or anyone else for that matter. I noticed a couple of colorful posters for rock albums by Journey and The Police, but no customers to buy them.

I was flipping through albums of Mozart piano concertos when I heard someone enter the store from a back room. I turned and saw a young man approaching me. It was Wes Boyer.

"Can I help you?" he asked, giving me a funny look, as though he knew me from somewhere but couldn't remember where. For Kay Boyer's son, he struck me as surprisingly unattractive. He was fairly tall, with curly brown hair like his sister's, but acne scars marred his skin, and his small gray eyes were cold.

"Just looking," I said. "You've got a pretty good collection of Mozart here."

"Oh, yeah," he nodded. "Mozart's one of my favorites, so I've got a lot of his stuff. Too much."

"You can never have too much Mozart," I said, forcing a smile. I was hoping he'd relax and talk to me.

"No? Looks like I have too much of everything."

"Business hasn't been too good lately?" The answer was obvious.

"Nope," he said sullenly. "This location stinks, for one thing. The only foot traffic we get is for the beauty shop next door. And you can guess how many ladies from the beauty shop come in here."

I nodded sympathetically. He was opening up more quickly than I'd hoped.

"And don't ask about the record business. Nobody's in great shape nowadays–unless you're a big chain like Music City." He clearly regretted his decision to open a small store like this one. "Those guys have the bucks to advertise. That generates business. They get the business and take it away from little guys like me. Just look." He waved his hand around the store. "Nothing. Just you and those kids. On a Saturday morning."

"Well, maybe things will pick up later. The teenagers are probably still sleeping."

"Maybe. I do get some teenage kids who want the latest records. But if business doesn't pick up by Christmas, I just may go belly-up."

"Really? That would be a shame."

The discussion was going nowhere. But how could I bring up his mother?

"Yeah," Wes said. He gave me that funny look again. "Say, don't I know you from somewhere?" My problem was about to be solved. "Did you know my mother? I saw you at the house yesterday. You came after the funeral, right?"

"Right," I said, nodding.

"And now you're here. Is that a coincidence, or what?"

"My kids wanted to look at records today, that's all," I said quickly. "I didn't mean to upset you. Look, I'll leave if you want me to." I was bluffing. I didn't think he'd want his only customers to walk out.

"No, no, that's all right," he said. "It just struck me as funny, that's all."

"I was very sorry about your mother's death," I said, trying to return to talking about his mother.

"Yeah, it was too bad, all right." He looked away from me and focused on the opposite wall. "She was a good person. She helped me get this store underway, you know."

"No, I didn't. But I know she was a wonderful person." I paused. "Your father, too." I watched for his reaction.

Wes looked back at me. "My father? Uh...Dad's always been a little off the wall." He smiled. "But you probably knew that already."

"I don't know your dad at all. I just met him yesterday, at the house. But he seemed devastated by your mother's death."

"Yeah. We all are." The smile had vanished.

"Your parents must have had a great marriage." Maybe this would inspire another reaction.

"Great? I wouldn't call it great," he said.

"You wouldn't?"

"Well, like any marriage, it probably was great to begin with. Hell, mine was, too. And look what happened to me. D-I-V-O-R-C-E," he twanged, his mouth twisted in an ironic half-smile.

"But their marriage...it didn't work out that well?"

He paused. "As I said, Dad's kind of peculiar. He inherited a little money, so he never had to work very hard. I don't think he ever held down a real job. He played a little golf years ago, before his heart started acting up. Otherwise, he hung around the house most of the time.

"My mother, she got all wrapped up in that school of hers. We didn't see a lot of her once she started the school. I was in high school by that time, and it didn't bother me. Me and my friends, we didn't want our mothers hovering over us anyway. But I think it probably bothered my sisters."

"Your sisters? They were upset that your mother wasn't around very much?"

"Yeah. Bree, especially. She was the youngest. Seven years younger than Julie." He paused again. "You know about Julie?"

I nodded.

"Yeah, well, Mom was never the same after Julie died. Got even more wrapped up in her school. Like she thought she could forget what happened if she was working all the time. It was pretty grim. I wasn't living at home anymore, but as far as I could tell, things went from bad to worse."

"How did your parents get along after that?"

"You mean after Julie died?"

I nodded.

"They drifted apart even more. But for some reason they stayed married. Dad developed a heart condition, and she probably thought she should stick around. But I never talked to her about it." He paused. "Maybe I should have."

The girls were still looking through the children's records, but I didn't know how long that would last. I had to shift gears. "Do you think Jack Hines killed her?"

He looked startled by the question. "Christ, I guess so," he said. "I really haven't thought about it. I just figured the cops know what they're doing."

"They usually do. But is there anybody else you think might have...?"

"Jeez, I don't know," he said, shaking his head. "I didn't see a lot of my folks lately. I haven't lived at home for a long time, not since I got married. I've kind of lost touch."

"So you can't think of anyone who might have wanted to harm your mother?"

He shook his head emphatically. "Oh, no. Everybody liked her." Then he hesitated for a moment. "My sisters had some problems with her. Hell, I did, too. But I don't think Bree ever hated her, not enough to want to hurt her." He cocked his head, looking at me more closely. "Why do you want to know anyway?"

Just then, Missy and Lindsay came running over. "Mommy, Mommy, I want this one," Lindsay shouted, waving the album from Walt Disney's "Cinderella" in my face.

"Okay, honey, you can get it," I said, turning to Wes Boyer with a smile.

"That's not fair!" Missy said. "I want one, too."

"Okay. Which one do you want?"

"I want 'Cinderella' too!"

"You and Lindsay can share this one," I said calmly, doing my mother-with-a-well-modulated-voice bit.

"No! I want my own!"

"That's impossible. Nobody buys two records that are exactly the same." My patience was wearing thin, and my voice was beginning to leave the well-modulated range.

Missy started to cry. She pulled the record out of Lindsay's hands. Now both of them were crying.

"Okay, we'll leave right now without any records," I said hotly.

"Wait a minute," Wes interrupted. "Come with me, girls. We'll find another one that's just as nice as 'Cinderella.'" He led the girls back to the children's section and helped them choose another Disney album, "Snow White."

Peace and harmony restored, I paid for both records.

"Thanks for the business," Wes said as we headed for the door. "Why don't you call Bree sometime? She's staying with my father right now."

Both girls tightly clutched their records as we climbed into the car. Somewhere in an animated heaven, Walt Disney must have looked down on us and smiled.

CHAPTER 17

As we passed the nursery school on our way home, Lindsay piped up. "Know what we did at school yesterday?"

"What?"

"Mrs. Thurgood passed out colored paper, and we made funny Halloween pictures. Mine's a scary monster with big green teeth," she giggled.

"Good, honey," I said absentmindedly. I was wondering what we'd have for lunch when we got home.

A minute later, I made myself remember what Lindsay had said, just in case it was something important. Sometimes I answered the kids' comments without really listening. I'd say "Uh-huh," then realize later I had no idea what they said.

I concentrated until I recalled what Lindsay had said. Nothing important. Just another art project at school.

But something about it bothered me. What was it?

I was fixing lunch ten minutes later when it registered. Mrs. Thurgood! I'd forgotten all about talking to her. Rella Cox had mentioned a serious argument Kay Boyer had with Betty Thurgood years ago. I wanted to know more about it.

I served lunch quickly, then checked some local phone books till I found a listing for an Elizabeth Thurgood on Woodridge Road in Glenview Park.

A reedy voice answered.

"This is Alison Ross, Lindsay's mother."

"Lindsay? Oh, you mean the little Lindsay in my afternoon class?"

"Yes, that's right."

"Is something wrong?"

"No, no, nothing's wrong. I was just wondering if I could drop in to talk to you this afternoon."

"Here, at my home?" she asked. "That's most unusual. Can't we meet at school on Monday?"

"I need to talk to you today. Please let me come by this afternoon." I could hear the pleading tone in my voice.

"Well, as I said, it's most unusual, but I suppose I wouldn't mind having a little company today," she said.

"Can I come right now?"

"That will be fine. Apartment 3-F." Betty Thurgood hung up.

I found Marv preparing some class notes for Monday. "I'd like to go out for a while," I said. "Would that be okay?

"Sure, sweetness." Marv agreed to take over the rest of the girls' lunch and amuse them while I was gone. Maybe he'd take them for a bike ride, he said.

I gave him a kiss, then hurried out of the house and into the Toyota, heading for Glenview Park, a mid-sized suburb on the other side of West Winnette.

Betty Thurgood lived in a small apartment complex just off Glenview Park Road. I rang the bell downstairs, was buzzed in, and took the elevator to the third floor. Her apartment door was already open when I reached it.

"Come in," she said, ushering me inside. On her small dinette table, a pot of coffee and a plate of cookies beckoned. I seated myself at the table and took a chocolate chip cookie while she poured the coffee. A jolt of caffeine would help me stay awake in the overheated apartment.

"Now why did you want to see me?" she asked, sitting down across from me. "Lindsay isn't having any trouble adjusting to a new teacher, is she?"

"Oh, no. Not at all," I assured her.

"Is she having problems with the other children?"

"No, nothing like that."

"Well, then, what is the reason for your visit?" She had a puzzled look on her heavily wrinkled face.

"It's...it's about Kay Boyer," I said.

"Kay Boyer? Why on earth would you want to talk to me about Kay?"

"I've been looking into the circumstances surrounding her murder, and Rella Cox suggested that I talk to you."

"Talk to *me*?" She looked indignant. "But what in the world could I possibly tell you?"

"Rella Cox told me that, years ago, you and Kay had a dispute, a dispute that led you to leave the nursery school. Can you tell me about it?"

"Are you suggesting...I can hardly believe my own ears! Are you suggesting I had something to do with Kay's death?" Betty's face had turned red, and her breathing was suddenly agitated.

"No, no, not at all," I said quickly. "I just thought...I thought you might know something about Kay...something that might help me find her killer."

"But the police have already arrested someone, that Hines fellow," she protested.

"Yes, I know. But I'm not convinced he did it."

She stared at me without speaking.

"Won't you please tell me what happened? It may be important."

Her face remained stony. I tried groveling. "Please, Mrs. Thurgood. What you have to say could make a big difference."

She kept staring at me for what seemed like a long time. Finally she spoke.

"Well, I don't know why you're mixed up in this, but I'll tell you what happened. It's history now, history, and I can't imagine what earthly good it will do to go over it again after so many years. But I have nothing to hide. Nothing to hide." She rose from her chair and began to pace back and forth as she talked.

"We had that argument, oh, about a dozen years ago. I'd started working at East Winnette at the very beginning, when Kay first opened the school. I think I was the first teacher she hired. Kay was the kind of mother who's restless staying at home, and she'd always worked part-time at one of the local nursery schools. Then, once her children were a little older, she started East Winnette Nursery School. She was terribly excited about being in charge of her very own school.

"We had a wonderful relationship. We loved working together. There was only one thing we didn't see eye-to-eye on, and that was Kay's family."

"Her family?"

"You see, I'm quite old-fashioned on this subject. Maybe too old-fashioned. I think it's important that parents spend time with their children, the young ones especially. But the older ones need attention, too. And Kay...Kay chose to ignore that."

Betty sat down across from me again. "I was a widow when I went back to work, and my children were grown. I had plenty of time to devote to my teaching. But Kay still had three children at home, and she began to spend very little time with them. She became obsessed with the school. She put in so many hours at that place—getting there early, leaving late, running programs in the evening and weekends, going to one teachers' conference after another. Then she got herself elected president of the North Shore Nursery School Teachers' League, and that took up even more of her time."

"But didn't she have sitters watch her children when she wasn't home?"

"The two older children didn't need sitters. They could look after themselves, and they watched their little sister. But all of them still needed attention from their parents, don't you see?

"They needed someone to be there after school now and then. And Kay was never there for them." She shook her head sadly.

"What about her husband?"

"Tom Boyer? Oh, he was probably around the house sometimes. I don't think he ever had a steady job, so he hung around the house quite a lot. But he wasn't the kind of father those kids needed. I don't think he paid any attention to them." She shook her head again.

"How did this lead to your argument with Kay?"

A wistful smile crept over her face. "It's funny, really. You know that line: 'Even your best friends won't tell you.' Well, I considered Kay one of my best friends, and I foolishly thought I *could* tell her what to do."

She suddenly looked solemn again. "Kay's relationship with her kids started bothering me. She admitted to me she was having problems with them, especially Julie, her older daughter. One day, when she brought up Julie's name again, I flew off the handle. I told her exactly what I thought of the way she was raising those kids. I said I wouldn't be surprised if her kids turned out to be juvenile delinquents, or worse.

"It was so ironic, really. Here was a woman who devoted herself to child-care, and she was neglecting her own children in order to spend time with other people's kids."

Betty's eyes had glazed over. She was reliving the argument that took place so long ago.

"And...?"

"And she blew up. She was livid, furious with me. She screamed and shouted, finally telling me to get out. She couldn't work with me any longer, she said. Of course, I knew it was her anxiety about those kids that was making her say it, but it was too late to patch things up. I resigned and found myself another job. That's when I moved out here to Glenview Park."

"And that's all there was to it?"

Betty paused. "Not quite all," she said. "A year or two later I read in the paper that Julie had committed suicide. *Suicide.* My heart broke for Kay." Betty's eyes suddenly filled with tears. "I went to the funeral, and I cried for dear little Julie. But I couldn't bring myself to go up to Kay. I knew I'd be a reminder of everything I'd said to her." She paused. Her head shook slowly back and forth. "I warned Kay. I tried to tell her...."

"Yes, you certainly did," I said. "You have nothing to feel guilty about...."

"Guilty?" Suddenly she seemed to remember who she was, and who I was. My use of the word "guilty" was clearly a blunder. "Certainly not," she huffed. "Kay's the one who's guilty, not me!"

"Yes, she is," I said. "I mean, was."

"Was," she repeated. "Was. Now Kay's gone, too. Murdered...." Her eyes began to glaze over again. "Murdered...."

"Well, thank you, Mrs. Thurgood," I said, getting up. "I'm really glad you could find time to talk to me today."

"Oh my yes," she said, her eyes focusing on me again. "I hope I've been of some help to you."

"Well, yes, you have," I lied. Our conversation hadn't really helped me very much. "By the way, we all feel very lucky you came back to the nursery school this week. I don't know what we would have done without you." I thought I might as well earn some Brownie points with her before I left.

"Oh, thank you, Mrs. Ross," she said, smiling. "I'm happy to do some teaching again until a permanent replacement can be found. I was actually quite pleased when Rella Cox called me. Being retired can get to be a bore, you know."

"So I've heard."

I understood how she felt. Although life at home with my daughters was busy, I was in a kind of professional retirement. A temporary one, at least.

I said goodbye and headed out the door.

Chalk one up for human interest, I thought. My trip to Glenview Park had been a waste. I hadn't learned anything that would help me solve Kay Boyer's murder.

Betty Thurgood certainly had an antiquated view of parenting. Even she admitted it. Not every parent was the sort to stay home all day, every day, with his or her kids. But maybe she was right to think Kay went too far in the other direction.

And maybe, even without Betty's criticism, Kay had felt guilty about neglecting her kids, especially after what happened to Julie. So what? Every parent feels guilty about something she did or didn't do.

But how did that relate to Kay's being murdered?

* * *

The house was silent when I returned. A big note on the fridge said "Out on our bikes."

I felt at loose ends and tried calling Judy's apartment. A breathless voice answered.

"Judy, is that you?"

"Who's this? Ali?"

"What's up? Your voice sounds funny."

"I was just doing aerobics. I've got this great new record— aerobic dancing with Jacki Sorensen. I just love it. Hold on– I'll turn it off."

Aerobics. A wave of jealousy briefly washed over me. I needed exercise badly. It was a constant struggle to keep my weight down, but I never seemed to have time to exercise. Maybe I needed to get a record like that.

"Ali? What's happening?"

"Well...the truth is, a lot's been happening."

"Tell me!"

"I've gotten involved in this murder case, the one I told you about the other day."

"Involved? What do you mean, involved?"

"I have a retainer to investigate the case."

"A retainer? From who?"

"From...from...." This was going to sound dumb. "From the mother of the guy the police have charged with the murder."

"The janitor? You took a retainer from his mother? Are you serious?"

"Now wait, Judy, it's not that crazy."

"Alison, I don't believe you're doing this! First, you find the body. Then you implicate the janitor. Now you're representing the janitor's mother while you do what? Try to prove he *didn't* do it?"

"I know it sounds kind of funny, but it...it's really not the way it sounds. I never said the guy did it, you know. All I said was that I saw him there. Then when his mother called, she pleaded with me, told me he's innocent, appealed to me as a mother to help him. What could I say?"

"You could have said 'no.'"

I didn't answer.

"Well, then, how much is she paying you to represent her?"

I couldn't tell Judy the truth. If I told her my retainer was a measly forty dollars, she'd laugh herself sick. "First of all, Judy, I'm not representing her. I'm not acting as her lawyer. I'm just making a few phone calls and talking to people, stuff like that."

"You didn't answer my question. How much?"

"I don't want to tell you that!" I was unhappy with the way this conversation was going. I'd called Judy to bounce some of my ideas off her. Instead she was bouncing my head against a brick wall.

"Okay, Ali, calm down. I withdraw the question." Lame lawyers' joke. "Just tell me whatever you want. I'll try to help any way I can."

I started to relax a little. "Okay, say this woman who was murdered was the director of a nursery school and she spent a lot of time there and didn't see much of her own kids. If some-one, an old friend maybe, accused her of neglecting her kids, and they had a fight and never saw each other again, do you see any connection between that and her murder?"

"Umm...not really. If anyone was angry, it was the direc-tor of the school, not the other way around."

"That's how I see it, too."

"Any other leads?"

"Nothing definite yet. But I have some other things to check out. Apparently the nursery school was about to be sold."

"That sounds promising."

"Yeah. I hope so." I couldn't think of anything else to run by Judy at the moment. "So what are you doing tonight?"

"I have a date with a prosecutor I met last week."

"Great! What's he like?" I wanted Judy to find someone. Someone like Marv. She loved her life, but I knew she sometimes thought about having a husband, maybe even kids, before she hit forty.

"I don't know him very well. Seems nice, as far as I can tell."

I heard the back door open. Next I heard the excited voices of Marv and the children. "Well, have a good time! Maybe we can have lunch sometime next week."

We agreed to try to meet for lunch, said our goodbyes, and returned to the two very distinct parts of the planet we inhabited.

CHAPTER 18

Saturday night Marv and I left the girls with a babysitter and went to a movie. After many false starts, I'd finally come up with a babysitter both Missy and Lindsay liked. Which meant we could leave the house without tears or screams emanating from either child.

The only problem arose when Marv and I wanted to go out, and Lynn, the only babysitter they both liked, was busy. We'd immediately mobilize in a desperate effort to come up with an appealing replacement. I sometimes had to make six or eight calls before I came up with one. And once in a while, if none of them panned out, we wound up staying home.

This is one of the many things they don't tell you *before* you have a baby.

Whenever possible, Saturday nights were reserved for Marv and me. I loved my children, but I also loved being alone with Marv. Sometimes we went to movies we suspected we wouldn't even like, just to have a chance to relate to each other without the kids.

This time we were lucky. "Body Heat" was still playing at a nearby theater. We both relished the clever plot and admired the riveting performances by sexy Kathleen Turner and hoodwinked William Hurt. The sexual tension in the film was palpable, and Marv grabbed my hand and held it tightly while we watched the stars make love on the big screen.

After the movie, we opted for a snack at a local deli, and I found myself telling Marv about Elmira Hines's forty-dollar retainer.

"Are you sure you want to get mixed up in this?" he asked. His gray-green eyes looked into mine with concern.

"No...," I answered slowly, "I'm not sure. But I think I want to try it for a while."

Marv hesitated, but he finally nodded. He understood how restless I felt sometimes, how eager I was to do something interesting with my time. Something I could do without leaving the kids at home with a nanny, or putting them into an all-day operation like Kidd's Korner.

"Well, try it then, sweetness, and see what happens," he said, grabbing my hand again and squeezing it in his. "I'll help you any way I can."

After Marv escorted Lynn home, we didn't follow our usual pattern of collapsing into bed at the end of a hectic day. We headed for bed, but with a considerably different approach.

As Marv walked through the door, I moved toward him with a seductive smile, and the game was on. Maybe seeing "Body Heat" was responsible. We certainly knew we wanted to have our own approximation of the sex-saturated scenes in the movie.

We started with gentle kissing but soon moved on to stripping our clothes off and planting more passionate kisses on each other's bodies. I felt him gently enter me, breathlessly murmuring in my ear, "I love you more than ever." We climaxed together and then covered each other with more kisses before separating, exhausted.

Climaxing together always made me think of the Beatles song, "Come Together," and in truth, a raft of Beatles songs had facilitated our romance. Marv had whispered "P.S. I Love You" to me in an L.A. parking lot, the first time either he or I dared to utter the word "love."

Making love with Marv was heaven, really. I couldn't help asking myself a question that always struck me after we made love. Why didn't we do it more often?

* * *

We fell sound asleep and hoped to stay in bed till eleven. Fools. By eight o'clock Sunday morning Lindsay was up and demanding breakfast. Marv managed to sleep through her demands, so I dragged myself out of bed and went downstairs.

An enormously fat Sunday *Tribune* beckoned, and as soon as I'd dispensed bowls of Cheerios to both girls, I succumbed to it. By ten o'clock, despite the racket the girls made while they colored and pasted Halloween decorations, I'd pushed myself through everything but the financial pages, the editorials, and the book reviews.

I needed a lower decibel level to absorb those three sections. When the girls finally got dressed and went outside to play in the back yard, I curled up with what remained of the paper.

I turned first to the book reviews and had just finished reading about Toni Morrison's latest when I spotted a review of Gabriel Kidd's book. I read it quickly. It summarized the book pretty much as I had while I waited in line at the bookstore.

But a couple of sentences in the review startled me: "Kidd's comet-like path to success has lately taken a downturn, as a quick glance at any recent *Wall Street Journal* will reveal.

Nevertheless, his book demonstrates the success, albeit transitory, a determined entrepreneur can achieve."

Kidd's success had suffered a downturn? It was now considered transitory? I dropped the book reviews and grabbed the financial pages. Sure enough, on page three I found a brief article noting "reverses in the day-care empire built by Gabriel Kidd," but not much more. I had to get to the library for more information. Unfortunately, it didn't open on Sundays until one o'clock.

I went upstairs to get dressed and was pulling on my socks when I remembered Bree Boyer. Her brother Wes had told me to call her. He seemed to think Bree had run into some problems with their mother, much more than he had. I wanted to talk to her.

Once again I looked up Kay Boyer's number in the school directory. I realized now that it must have been Bree who'd answered the phone Monday night. And now, less than a week later....

How much her life had changed since then. And mine.

The phone rang for a long time, but no one answered. I decided to drive by the Boyer house on my way to the library and see whether anyone was home.

We all sat down for a late breakfast and consumed stacks of Marv's famous French toast and scrambled eggs. Then, as one o'clock approached, Marv and the girls left for a movie, and I drove the Toyota to the Boyers' home. I climbed the crumbling steps once more and rang the bell several times. After a few minutes, Bree Boyer came to the door.

She gave me a puzzled look.

"Hi, Bree." I said quickly. "It's Alison Ross. From the nursery school."

It took her a minute to remember who I was. Finally she said, "Oh, hi. How are you?" She stayed by the door, clearly unwilling to welcome me inside.

"Fine, thanks," I said. "Umm...Bree, do you think we could talk for a few minutes?"

"Now?" she asked. "Why?"

"I want to talk to you about your mother, Bree. If you're busy today, could I come by tomorrow?"

"What?" She scowled at me. "Why do you want to talk to me? I don't...."

"Let me explain," I interrupted. "I'm trying to find out who murdered your mother. It may not have been Jack Hines. I want to ask you some...."

"Wait a minute." Now she was the one who interrupted. "I don't know why you're doing this, and I don't care. But don't expect me to talk to you about your little project. I have better ways to spend my time!" She shut the door in my face.

It took me a minute to process what had just happened. Why was Bree unwilling to talk to me? Why had she closed the door on me so abruptly? She'd seemed in pretty good shape when I met her after her mother's funeral.

Was she now in shock, delayed shock, from her mother's death, unwilling to touch what was still a raw wound? Or was she trying to hide something? Something that might be important. But what?

Bree Boyer wouldn't have killed her own mother. Or would she?

I climbed back into the Toyota and headed for the East Winnette Public Library. I found a spot in the parking lot and pulled in.

Just outside the library's entrance I saw Nancy Singer approaching me. My heart sank.

Nancy was a lawyer I'd met at the nursery school three years earlier, when her son Brian was in Missy's class. She'd let everyone know she had no intention of being a stay-at-home mom much longer. At the annual holiday party for parents and children, she took me aside to tell me how much she missed working and how she couldn't wait to go back. Sometime later that year she'd returned to full-time work at her former law firm. I hadn't seen her since.

I couldn't face talking to Nancy and tried to avoid her by focusing on my sneakers. Then I heard "Alison!" and knew there was no escape.

"How *are* you, Alison? Haven't seen you in ages! Are you working yet?" Nancy was enveloped in a long fur coat. It looked incongruous with the Levi's that were peeking out from underneath the fur.

"I'm working, Nancy. I consider what I do *work*."

"I mean legal work, Alison."

"Right. Well, you know, Nancy, I've tried to find something part-time, but nothing's turned up yet."

"Oh, yes, part-time," Nancy said, nodding. "I remember your talking about that. Hard to find, though."

"Yes, it is."

"Well, I know my schedule isn't for everyone. I'm exhausted all the time. But I can't imagine staying home all day. Aren't you bored?"

"Not really." I couldn't admit to her that there were some boring moments at home with the girls. But she was right about her schedule. It wasn't for everyone. Certainly not for me.

"How's Brian?" I asked. I genuinely wondered how he was doing now that Nancy was working such long hours.

"Umm…Brian's doing just fine," she answered. "We hired a nanny."

"Does she live with you?"

"Uh-huh," Nancy nodded. "That way she's there when I leave for work, and she's there when I get home, no matter how late it is. It works out great."

"Well, I'm glad that's working out for you, Nancy. I don't think I could handle it."

"Have to run, Alison. Great to see you!" Nancy turned and dashed off, her fur coat flapping as she went.

It wasn't really cold enough for fur, and I wouldn't have worn fur even if it were, but the luxurious long coat seemed emblematic of the different paths Nancy and I had chosen. I was perfectly happy in my jeans jacket, and happy—for the moment—at home with my kids. I knew that if I tried working full-time like Nancy, struggling to fit some time with my kids into a 60-hour work-week, I'd have bleeding ulcers to go along with that fur coat. No thanks.

I headed for the library's reference room and began leafing through copies of the *Wall Street Journal* in hopes of finding something about Kidd's Korner. Although I didn't understand all the financial jargon, I remembered enough corporate law terminology about stocks and bonds to grasp most of it.

My search led to two articles about Gabriel Kidd. One stated that his company had run into problems trying to buy schools in the eastern half of the country after saturating the market on the West Coast. The other article was even more revealing.

According to the *Journal*, Kidd's cash flow was in serious trouble, and he'd stopped offering cash to the schools he wanted to buy. Instead, he was offering stock in his company, appraised at a value the *Journal* described as "inflated." As a result, Kidd's overtures were being rejected by most of the schools he approached. The *Journal* predicted difficult times ahead for Kidd's Korner.

I was stunned. When I'd met him on Friday, Gabriel Kidd had been the consummate business executive, confident, exuding power. Now I began to see him in a new light. He was in trouble, his company teetering on financial stilts that were about to give way. All that talk about the deal he'd made with Kay Boyer—it couldn't have been true. Maybe he'd promised her a lot of money, but by the time they were ready to sign a contract, he had no cash to give her.

Kay wouldn't have traded her precious school for a load of worthless stock in Kidd's faltering company. Then what had really happened between them?

"Alison?"

I looked up. Who was this good-looking guy leaning over me? Intense blue eyes, curly brown hair, a lopsided smile. The total package reminded me of Paul Newman in "Butch Cassidy."

"You're Alison Ross, aren't you?"

I nodded. His clear blue eyes locked mine.

"I'm Neal. Neal Bannister. Mary Beth's husband. I think we've met once or twice."

Blurry scenes of Hot Dog Day at the nursery school raced through my head. Frantic parents, screaming babies, wild three- and four-year-olds tugging at our legs while we exchanged names.

"Right. I remember meeting you." A face like his you don't easily forget.

"Mary Beth told me about you and Mrs. Boyer. Then I saw that article in the *Trib*. Has all that settled down by now?"

"Pretty much. Things are mostly back to normal." I wasn't about to mention my new role to someone like Neal.

"Good," he nodded. He grabbed the chair next to me and sat down. "So what are you up to here?"

"Not much. I was...."

A librarian hurried over. It was the heavyset blonde who was awfully hostile for a librarian. I'd had run-ins with her before.

"I'm sorry, but this room is not for socializing. If you want to talk, you'll have to move outside."

I looked at Neal. He looked at me. "Want to have a cup of coffee someplace?" he asked.

"Sure."

We walked up the street to Bill's Snack Shop, located across from the commuter train station. It turned out to be closed on Sunday, so we kept walking, heading for Palmer Brothers' Pancake House three blocks farther.

"Won't Mary Beth wonder where you are?" I asked.

"She took the kids to see her mother this afternoon. Her mom's in a nursing home, and I find it kind of depressing, so I begged off today. Mary Beth understands how I feel."

Mary Beth was the understanding type. She'd no doubt understand why Neal and I were going somewhere for coffee together, wouldn't she?

The pancake house was crowded. Its wood-paneled-and-stained-glass decor had welcomed East Winnette pancake mavens for decades. Hollywood types had even descended on the place to shoot a movie scene there. Now, as always, noisy patrons were devouring the world's best apple pancakes and pecan waffles, and washing it all down with cup after steaming cup of freshly-brewed coffee.

The hostess ushered Neal and me to a small booth, and we ordered coffee and one gigantic apple pancake to share. He asked again what I'd been doing in the library's reference room.

"Have you ever heard of Kidd's Korner?" I asked.

"The chain of day-care centers?"

"Right. I heard that the owner is interested in buying East Winnette Nursery School, and I was just checking up on him and what kind of business he runs."

"I didn't realize you were interested in business, Alison. Have you worked in the business world?"

"Not exactly. I'm trained as a lawyer, but I never worked in a corporation myself."

"But you're interested in it now?"

"Well, I'm interested in the nursery school...how it would be affected if Kidd's Korner took over, that sort of thing."

"But now that Kay Boyer's dead, will the deal still go through?"

"I...I don't know. I guess her husband has the right to sell it. I met him on Friday, but he struck me as too upset to talk about it."

Neal nodded.

"Anyway, what I learned in the library is that Kidd's Korner isn't in great shape financially right now. So I don't know whether it would still be in Tom Boyer's interest to sell to Gabriel Kidd."

"Hey, you sound really caught up in all this," Neal laughed. "I had no idea."

I had to laugh, too. "I guess I do sound awfully involved. Let's change the subject."

"Okay." Blue eyes pierced mine. "What do you want to talk about?"

I couldn't think of a thing. His looks rattled me. I felt like a teenaged schoolgirl on a date with the class hunk, and my heart was beating much faster than normal. "Uh...well, tell me what *you* do. Are you in business?"

"Securities."

"Oh." That sounded dull, very un-Neal-like. I had pictured him as, say, an architect, designing wildly dramatic houses perched on cliffs, something like that.

"Yeah. I got an M.B.A. and decided to go into securities when it still seemed like a fairly profitable thing to do. Now that the market has changed, I sometimes wonder if I made the right choice." He looked troubled.

Our apple pancake arrived, and we dug in. It was steaming hot, and the apples and cinnamon encrusted on top had caramelized to perfection.

"If you're in securities, maybe you could look into Kidd's Korner," I said. "And Gabriel Kidd. I came across a couple of articles in the *Wall Street Journal*, but you could probably find out much more than I did."

"I can certainly try."

"Great," I said between bites.

We finished eating and got up to leave Palmer Brothers. On the way out, I thought I saw Rella Cox in a booth in the back, seated next to another older woman. She seemed totally absorbed in whatever her companion was was saying.

Someone who looked like Andrea Lewis was in another booth, watching Neal and me as he paid the bill. (My pleas to go Dutch treat had fallen on deaf but adorable ears.) I waved at Andrea, got no reaction, and thought maybe I was mistaken.

Neal insisted on walking me to my car in the library parking lot. As I started the engine, he leaned toward me. "I'll give you a call if I find out anything."

"Thanks. That'll be great." My hands were shaking a little as I drove away. I was a happily married woman. Why was my heart suddenly pounding?

When I got home, Marv was already fixing dinner, preparing *coq au vin*, one of his specialties. My kids had to be the only ones in East Winnette who regularly feasted on *coq au vin*.

"Umm! The food smells great! Where are the girls?" It was strangely quiet on the first floor.

"Missy's in her room reading," Marv said. "And Lindsay is listening to records, I think. Did you accomplish anything in the library?"

"I think so. Tell you about it later." I wasn't ready to tell Marv anything that had happened that afternoon. Not just yet. Instead I tiptoed upstairs to look in on the girls.

Lindsay's room was at the top of the stairs. I opened the door a crack. She was seated next to her tiny record player, listening to "Cinderella," a rapt expression on her face.

Walt, I thought, you've done it again. Another new fan, years after your demise.

I decided to interrupt. "Lindsay, Mommy's home!" Lindsay looked up with a big smile.

"Hi, Mommy!" she shouted. Together we got Missy and went downstairs for dinner.

CHAPTER 19

Monday morning dawned bright and sunny, a perfect autumn day. Marv and Missy went off to school, and Lindsay and I were heading outside for a visit to the local tot-lot when the kitchen phone rang. It was Jack Hines.

"Alison Ross?" His voice was husky. "I just got your message."

I pictured him as he spoke. His prominent jaw, the tousled hair, the cinnamon suede jacket....

"One minute," I said. I put down the phone and persuaded Lindsay to play in the back yard for a while. I could keep an eye on her through the kitchen window while I talked.

"Mr. Hines," I said when I got back to the phone, "do you know who I am?"

"They told me you're one of my lawyers, but you...aren't you the lady who saw me at the nursery school?" he said hesitantly.

"That's right."

"So what are you doing calling me?"

"Well...," I said, "your mother called me last week."

"My mother? She called you?"

"Yes. She told me you were innocent."

"Oh?" He sounded surprised. "Well, yeah, I am."

"She asked me to help you."

"She did?" He sounded even more surprised. "Well, are you gonna do it?"

"I'll try to...for a little while, anyway."

"Sounds good to me. I can use all the help I can get."

"I'm sure you can. I called to ask you a few questions."

"Oh, yeah? Like what?"

"Well, I've been talking to a lot of people, and...."

"What people?" he asked gruffly.

"Some people here in East Winnette."

"What'd you find out?" Hines's tone was becoming more insistent, more demanding.

"Nothing yet, but I'm working on it. You have to be patient."

"Patient!" The polite veneer with which he'd begun our conversation was now completely eroded. "I'm in jail, charged with murder!"

"Look, I'm doing the best I can. I'm not a professional detective, you know." I didn't mention that I was a lawyer, but I suddenly remembered to ask him about his. "Have you talked to your lawyer? Did you tell him you're innocent?"

"Of course, I did!" Hines said. "The kid's okay, he said he'll do what he can, but look, he got a hundred other cases, so how much can he do? Maybe now, if I tell him you're working on my case, he'll...."

"What?" I interrupted.

"I said, if I tell him you're working on my case, maybe he...."

"Wait, don't tell him that," I blurted out. I had visions of being called up before a committee on legal ethics. I wasn't sure what the canons of ethics said about what I was doing.

"Why? Is there something wrong with that?" he asked.

"I don't know for sure," I said. "I don't think so. But don't mention it to your lawyer right now. Or anybody else.

Okay?" Even if my investigation into the murder was ethical, I wasn't ready to let everyone know about it.

"Okay, okay," he said. "If that's how you want it. Just remember, the police arrested the wrong guy. You gotta remember that! I don't want to fry while the real guy gets off scot-free."

"I know that. Look, I've found out a lot already, I really have. And if I can just talk to Mrs. Boyer's daughter.... I think she knows something...."

"Then talk to her!" he interrupted. "What's the problem?"

"It's not that easy. I'm doing what I can, believe me."

"Okay, okay," he said. "I appreciate what you're doing. But you gotta understand my situation. I don't like being cooped up in this jail while the real guy's walking around out-side."

I suddenly remembered the questions I wanted to ask him. "Listen, Jack...can I call you Jack?"

"Sure."

"What were you doing at the nursery school that morn-ing?"

"I went to pick up my jacket," he answered. "I got this new jacket, it cost me a bundle. I didn't want some kids put-ting their dirty hands all over it."

"You left the jacket there the day before?"

"Yeah, that's right. So I went over that morning to get it before school started."

"Did you see Mrs. Boyer there?"

"I didn't see nobody. Except you."

"You didn't see anyone else around the building—besides me?"

"I already told you," he said impatiently. "I didn't see nobody."

"Okay, Jack. What about the petty cash?"

"What cash?"

"The petty cash." I wasn't sure myself what I was asking about. It figured that the nursery school would have some petty cash, but I certainly didn't know where it was kept.

"You mean that money they had in that metal box? In that Ms. Cox's desk?"

"Yes," I guessed.

"Did that Cox bitch tell you I took money out of that box?"

That Cox bitch? Maybe Rella's view of Jack Hines was right on target.

"Not exactly," I said. "But I think she suspects that you took it."

"Yeah...I took a couple bucks from it once or twice, just to tide me over till payday," he said. "I meant to put it back. But I always forgot."

"I see."

"But that don't make me a killer. Just 'cause I took a couple bucks now and then don't mean I killed nobody!"

"I know it doesn't, Jack. Calm down," I said. "I just had to know, that's all."

"Okay, okay," he said. "That Ms. Cox, she always had it in for me, ever since I started working there. But that don't mean I'm guilty of murder."

"I know, Jack." I glanced outside. Lindsay had begun digging up dirt with her tiny shovel and redistributing it all over the back yard. Her face was already streaked with mud. "Listen, Jack, I've got to go. I'll talk to you again soon." I hung up and headed outside.

I managed to get Lindsay out of the yard, cleaned up, and deposited in the living room with our big box of Legos by eleven o'clock. I looked at my watch and computed California time in my head. Nine o'clock. I figured the corporate head-quarters of Kidd's Korner should be open by now.

I found Gabriel Kidd's business card in my purse and dialed his number. Kidd's Korner offices were located in the seaside town of La Jolla. Jeez, I thought, if I were a CEO who could set up my headquarters anywhere I wanted, I'd choose La Jolla, too.

Marv and I had spent an idyllic year in La Jolla the year Missy was born. He'd been a visiting professor at the univer-sity, and I'd managed to scrounge up a part-time teaching job at a local law school.

I pictured La Jolla—the Cove, the beaches, the chic little shops—while I waited for someone to answer the phone.

"Good morning, this is Kidd's Korner," a harried voice finally answered.

"Gabriel Kidd, please."

"I'm sorry, Mr. Kidd is out of town," the voice said. "I'll put you through to his secretary."

A moment later another voice came on the line. "This is Sharon Stem, Mr. Kidd's secretary. Can I help you?"

"Ms. Stem, my name is Alison Ross. I met Mr. Kidd here in Chicago last week, and he gave me this number. He said I should get in touch with him if...if I wanted to talk to him again."

"Well, Mr. Kidd is out of town right now. He's still on tour promoting his new book. Maybe I can help you."

"I don't know if you can. Mr. Kidd and I were discuss-ing the death of a Mrs. Kay Boyer." No reaction. "She owned a nursery school here in East Winnette, and Mr. Kidd was interested in buying it. Kay...Kay was found murdered last Tuesday."

"Oh, I remember that incident now," Ms. Stem said. "Mr. Kidd gets all the large metropolitan dailies, and I saw the story about Kay Boyer in the Chicago paper. I thought the name sounded familiar, so I mentioned it to Mr. Kidd. He was quite upset about it."

"Yes, he was." I wasn't sure how to proceed from there.

"What did you want to discuss with Mr. Kidd today?" Ms. Stem was beginning to lose patience with me.

"I was just wondering where Mr. Kidd was earlier last week. Last Monday and Tuesday?"

"Mr. Kidd? He was still in La Jolla, I think. Let me check his calendar." She paused while she checked it. "No, I stand corrected. He left on the book tour Monday night. His first appearance was in Detroit at noon on Tuesday."

"I see."

"Was there anything else you wanted to know?" she asked briskly, making clear that she had a hundred things to do that were more important than talking to me.

"Well, I've been wondering about Mr. Kidd's financial situation, how that might have affected his dealings with Kay Boyer. Is it true he's stopped paying cash for the schools he buys, that he now offers stock in his company instead of cash?"

"I'm afraid I can't divulge that kind of information. I'm not at liberty to discuss details of Mr. Kidd's financial transactions. But I can take a message and ask him to get back to you on that."

"Oh...all right. Will you please tell him I called and ask him to call me back?" I gave her my name and number and hung up.

Very interesting. Gabriel Kidd had left California Monday night and flown to Detroit for an appearance at noon Tuesday. Just enough time for a quick stopover in Chicago at eight o'clock Tuesday morning.

CHAPTER 20

I dropped Lindsay off at the nursery school at 12:30 and headed back home. I wanted to try finding Bree Boyer again. I had no idea where she'd be on a Monday afternoon–maybe at the business college her father mentioned–but I figured I'd start by phoning the house again. I called the number—by this time I was beginning to know it by heart–but once again I got no answer.

I was thinking about calling Judy and making a date for lunch when my phone rang.

"Is this Alison Ross?" asked a woman's voice.

"Yes, it is."

"You don't know me, but I read about you in the paper, and I want you to know that...that...you identified the wrong man," the voice said.

"What?"

"I said you identified the wrong man. At least I think so."

"What makes you think so?"

"Oh, I couldn't tell you that."

"Why not?" Come on, lady, I thought. If you have something to tell me, tell it.

"Well...I just couldn't, that's all."

I was beginning to get annoyed. "Look, I don't know who you are or why you're calling me, but if all you have to say is that I identified the wrong man, you're not helping me. Do you have anything else to say? If not, I'm going to hang up and forget you ever called me."

The woman didn't respond. After a minute, I decided to prod her some more.

"Look...," I started, but she interrupted me.

"All right," she said. "I'll tell you what I know. But I don't want to do it over the phone. Can I meet you someplace?"

"Sure. Where?"

"Someplace where there aren't a lot of people. Where I won't see anybody I know."

I thought for a moment. "How about Sheridan Park?"

"Sheridan Park?" She sounded dubious.

"Do you have a car?"

"Yes."

"I'll meet you in the parking lot by the beach, near the Coast Guard station. There aren't many people there this time of year."

She hesitated. Finally she said "All right. I know the spot you mean. I can be there in ten minutes."

"So can I. I drive a brown Toyota. And I have red hair."

"I have a blue Chevy." She hung up.

I left the house and headed for the park. Sheridan Park is one of East Winnette's jewels—an emerald-green oasis filled with grass and huge old trees, bordered by a sandy beach. I drove up Sheridan Road and entered the park near the Coast Guard station, taking the road that went to the beach.

Only one other car–an empty black Mercedes—was parked at the beach when I got there. I parked the Toyota a few spaces from the Mercedes and began to watch for the blue Chevy.

The beach and the sky, the shoreline, even in autumn, were breathtakingly beautiful. The lake was a dark blue, and big whitecaps raced toward the shore in a steady, soothing tempo.

This stretch of beach always reminded me of one in La Jolla, the one Marv and I loved best the year we lived there. Sheridan Park Beach was possibly the only place in the entire Midwest that even came close to anywhere in La Jolla.

I heard a car pull up. I turned and saw the blue Chevy park next to the Toyota. A woman in her late 50s or early 60s emerged from it a moment later. Her hair, worn in a short bob, was dark black. It had to be dyed. I always wondered why many older women seemed to think that unnaturally dark hair made them look younger. It didn't.

She was wearing a purple polyester knit pantsuit that had gone out of style at least ten years before, but her body was trim and the pantsuit looked pretty good on her. She walked towards me hesitantly, as though she still wasn't sure she should be there.

I approached her with a friendly smile, hoping to put her at ease. "I'm Alison Ross," I called out. "Did you want to talk to me?"

She stopped walking and waited for me to reach her. "Yes, yes, I did," she said. "But now I don't know if I should...." Her small dark eyes darted back and forth, unwilling to focus on me.

"Well, why don't you tell me why you called? It must have been important, or you wouldn't have called me."

"Yes, yes, it is important." She looked down at her shoes. They were high-heeled black patent pumps, an odd match for her casual pantsuit.

"It's about Kay Boyer's death, isn't it?" I prompted. I couldn't put up with this stalling much longer.

The woman began to walk down the path along the beach. Feeling irritated, I walked alongside. If she had something to say, why didn't she say it?

After a moment she took a deep breath and began to talk. "My name is Thelma Eisenmayer," she said. "I used to work for Dr. Durkin."

"Dr. Durkin? The pediatrician?" Frank Durkin was a pediatrician with a successful practice in East Winnette, working out of a storefront office in the middle of the downtown business section.

"Yes," she said. "I worked for him for six years. I was his receptionist. And I was a very good receptionist. A pediatrician's receptionist does a lot more than answer the telephone, you know."

She was beginning to ramble, but I thought I'd let her have her say. If I interrupted her, she might clam up again.

"I had to know when to put a call through to the doctor, and when not to," she continued. "I would talk to worried parents on the phone and try to figure out what was wrong with their kids. I had to keep everyone in the waiting room happy, and try to keep the sick kids away from the healthy ones. There was a lot to that job, you know."

"Yes, I'm sure there was." Frankly, I doubted it. If I went by my own experiences in pediatricians' offices, the receptionists never seemed to care about their jobs as much as Thelma Eisenmayer claimed to.

"I put a lot of myself into that job," she went on. "It wasn't just answering phones. I had to..."

"Thelma," I interrupted. This had gone on long enough. "May I call you Thelma?" She nodded. "This is all very interesting. But you called me about Kay Boyer."

She hesitated again.

"Please tell me why you called."

"Well, I think someone should know." She paused.

"Know what?" This woman was driving me crazy.

"About Mrs. Boyer and...Dr. Durkin," she said.

"What is there to know?"

"They were lovers," she said.

Lovers? My face must have registered the shock I felt because she went on, "Oh, yes, my dear. They were lovers."

This *was* important.

"How did you find out about it?" I asked.

"Oh, I was in on it from the beginning. About two or three years ago, Mrs. Boyer invited Dr. Durkin to be on a panel over at the nursery school. For a discussion of children's illnesses."

I nodded. Kay Boyer had frequently organized "parents' nights" at the nursery school. She'd corral experts on child development, psychology, medicine, that sort of thing, and feature them at evening sessions at the school. I'd gone to a couple of them myself. I didn't remember one with Dr. Durkin, but it was logical that he would have shown up at some point.

"The two of them must have hit it off right away because a little while later she started calling him at the office, and he started making excuses to get away in the afternoon."

"In the afternoon?"

"Yes, about three-thirty or four o'clock. And there was chaos when he'd take off. That's the busiest time of day in a pediatrician's office."

I nodded again, remembering all the late afternoon visits I'd paid to Charlotte Henry, our pediatrician. Somehow a kid who seems perfectly okay at breakfast can be a cranky, feverish, sore-throated pain-in-the-ass by three or four o'clock in the afternoon, and the two of you wind up sitting in a hot, overcrowded waiting room filled with other cranky, feverish, sore-throated pains-in-the-ass until you get in to see the doctor.

"Of course," she said, "I was the one who had to deal with all the angry parents when he'd walk out. But he knew what he was doing. And he didn't care. All he wanted was to get his hands on Kay Boyer."

Thelma's pale face flushed a deep pink. She looked away for a moment. Then she regained her composure and began talking again. "This went on for a long time. She would call, and he would drop everything and run out of the office. But the past couple months, he didn't run so fast."

"Oh?"

"No," she said. "I overheard some of their conversations. At least his end of the line. And he started telling her he couldn't get away.

"Lately he was doing this more and more, and she was starting to get mad. I could tell from the tone of her voice when she'd call him. Sometimes he'd brush her off, and she'd call right back. She was fuming when she'd call back."

Kay Boyer fuming? Kay Boyer fuming because her lover was rejecting her? All of this was a bit hard to swallow. It just didn't jibe with the Kay Boyer I knew. Or thought I knew.

Thelma had stopped walking, so I stopped too. She turned to me and began to talk again. "Last Monday afternoon, about four o'clock, she called again, and he hung up on her pretty fast. Then he came out to my desk and told me not to put through any more of her calls. She called back right away, right after he told me that, and I told her what he said. She starting yelling at me, like it was my fault. So I told her I was just repeating what he told me." She stopped for a moment. "That's when she said it."

"Said what?"

"She said he'd better get his ass over there right away or he'd be sorry. Those were her exact words. She said he'd be sorry."

Another disconnect with the Kay Boyer I'd known. It raised a host of questions. "Do you know where she was calling from?" I asked.

"No. I never did. When she first started calling him, I thought she was calling from the nursery school. But later on, she maybe was calling from someplace else."

"What made you think that?"

"Well, once I realized what was going on, I just couldn't believe she'd be calling him from the school. And he'd run out so fast, he must have been going somewhere to be with her. It couldn't have been at the school, could it?" she asked.

"I don't know," I said. I tried to imagine a spot in the nursery school where they might have had their trysts, but I couldn't think of any place private enough. Kay Boyer had an office, but it was small and crowded and right next door to a classroom. "What happened next?"

"I told her I'd give him that message, and when he was between patients I told him. He muttered something under his breath. Something like 'That bitch.'" Thelma's face blushed again. "Then he just went on seeing patients. A few minutes later she called back. I told her I didn't think he was planning to leave the office. About fifteen minutes later she walked in."

"She walked into your office?"

"Yes," Thelma said. "She walked right in and demanded to see him. She came behind the desk and pulled me away, to talk to me in private. I guess she didn't want any of the mothers in the waiting room to recognize her. 'I want to see Frank,' she kept saying. Her teeth were clenched, and I could tell she was furious."

"Did he see her?"

Thelma nodded. "He finally saw her in one of the examining rooms. The one all the way in the back. Maybe he expected her to give him a hard time, that's why he put her back there."

"Did she?"

"Did she what?"

"Give him a hard time?"

Thelma nodded again. "They started arguing, and it got pretty loud. I was afraid the other patients would hear them, so I went back there to tell them to lower their voices. But... but I never went in."

"Why not?"

Thelma hesitated. Finally she spoke again. "When I got to the door, I heard such terrible things, I just couldn't go in there."

"What kind of terrible things?"

"She...she was telling him he was a bastard, and if he left her, she'd tell his wife everything."

"His wife? Dr. Durkin is married?"

"He's been married almost 35 years. They have their 35th anniversary next June." I must have looked skeptical because she added, "He had me keep track of things like that."

"What did he say when she threatened to go to his wife?"

"He said, 'Go ahead, I don't give a damn. You and I both know she doesn't care. She knows I see other women.' And then Mrs. Boyer said, in a queer voice, 'But what about the parents of your little patients? Do *they* know?' That's all I heard. I walked away. I just couldn't listen anymore."

Thelma looked out at the lake for a moment. Then she looked back at me. "After a few more minutes, she walked out. She left the office without saying anything. She looked like she could kill him."

She didn't kill him, I thought. But maybe he killed her.

"That's really interesting, Thelma," I said. "Thanks for telling me."

"Sure." She looked relieved that her ordeal was over. "I'm glad I told you. I thought someone should know."

"You're going to tell this to the police, aren't you?"

"The police?" She looked startled. "Oh, no, I don't want to tell the police. You tell them."

"The police should hear this directly from you."

"No, no, I don't want to have anything to do with the police," she said, shaking her head vigorously. The dyed black bob swayed back and forth. "You tell them." She started to walk towards her blue Chevy.

"Okay, Thelma, I'll tell them," I said. "But they'll probably want to question you after I do."

Thelma stopped walking and looked at me. "I thought it would be enough if I told you. I don't like policemen, I don't want to talk to them. Now I'm sorry I told you anything."

Her composure was crumbling. What experience in her past had made her so unwilling to talk to the police?

"I won't tell the police, not right away, Thelma, if you tell me something else."

"What's that?" She looked at me suspiciously, her small dark eyes half-closed.

"Why did you decide to talk to me? Do you think Dr. Durkin had something to do with Kay Boyer's murder?"

"I...I don't know," she stammered. She looked at the lake again. "But if he did, then that other man's innocent, isn't he?" She looked back at me.

I nodded. If Durkin killed Kay Boyer, Jack Hines was clearly innocent.

Thelma began walking toward her car again. I walked alongside her. Another question was nagging at me. "I'm also wondering why you're telling me all this about Dr. Durkin. You've been working for him for so long. Don't you feel something like...like loyalty to him?"

Thelma laughed. "Loyalty? After what he did to me, I don't feel a shred of loyalty!"

"What did he do to you?"

"He fired me," she said. "He fired me last week, two days after Mrs. Boyer was murdered."

I remembered now. She'd spoken of her employment with Durkin in the past tense.

"Why did he fire you?" Why would Durkin fire his receptionist of six years? And why did he do it the very same week that his lover was killed? Was it just a crazy coincidence? Or was there something connecting the two events?

"He told me his cousin needed a job, and he felt an obligation to help her out, so he was going to give her my job, starting this week. Can you believe it? After six years, he fires me and gives my job to a cousin!"

Another statistic to add to the latest unemployment figures. At her age, Thelma could have a tough time finding a new job.

"So now I'm out of work, with only two weeks' severance, and his cousin is sitting in my chair as his receptionist. I don't owe that man any loyalty at all."

Thelma and I had reached the spot where we parked our cars. She hurried into her Chevy and drove off before I could say anything else.

So Kay Boyer had had a lover. And her lover wasn't just anyone. He was one of East Winnette's most popular pediatricians. She'd created a scene in his office, and he broke off their relationship the day before she was murdered.

Had Kay Boyer angered Frank Durkin enough to kill her?

CHAPTER 21

It was nearly two o'clock when I drove out of Sheridan Park, trying to process the new information I'd just gotten from Thelma Eisenmayer. I wasn't sure what to do with it, but if I was going to do anything, I didn't have much time before the girls came home from school.

I found myself driving to the East Winnette business district and Frank Durkin's office. My chances of getting in to see him were probably slim, but I decided to try.

His office was in familiar territory. Downtown East Winnette, a collection of small shops and offices, wasn't far from my house. I'd often peered through the office window when I walked past it, en route to the bank or the post office. I'd noticed toys and children's books scattered around a small waiting room, and I'd sometimes thought how convenient it would be to take my children there instead of Charlotte Henry's office in Evanston. But I was too committed to Charlotte, a delightful combination of medical expertise and personal charm, to ever switch.

I parked in front of Hannah's, East Winnette's second-best bakery, and walked towards Durkin's office, trying to ignore the delicious smells emanating from the bakery. As I walked, I realized that the office was a short distance from the nursery school—just down the street and around the corner. The proximity must have been convenient for Kay Boyer. But then I wasn't sure exactly where she and Frank Durkin had held their rendezvous.

I entered the office and approached the receptionist's desk. The young woman seated there was clearly outside her normal surroundings. She was no more than 25, with an elaborate platinum blonde hairstyle and a flashy, form-fitting electric blue dress, both more suited to Dolly Parton than a pediatrician's receptionist in East Winnette.

She also appeared to be totally incompetent. Three weary mothers were hovering over her desk, trying to get her attention while she attempted to field two phone calls at the same time. Two small children in the waiting room were crying, adding to the already frantic atmosphere.

This must be the cousin Durkin told Thelma about, I thought. How stupid he was to fire Thelma and replace her with this dolt. I waited my turn as patiently as I could, glancing repeatedly at my watch while I waited. When the three mothers were finally dealt with, she turned to me.

"Can I help you?" she asked, sounding as though she didn't give a damn if she could or not.

"I need to speak to Dr. Durkin." I tried to inject a note of urgency into my voice.

"The name of your child?" she asked.

"I'm not here about my child. I have to...."

"You're not here about your child?" A vacant look of noncomprehension spread across her face.

"No. This is a personal matter," I said.

"A personal matter?" Now she looked totally bewildered. "I'll have to check with the doctor. Your name, please?" I told her, adding that it was urgent that I speak to him immediately. She nodded vacantly, and I took a seat in the waiting room.

It was, like all pediatrician's waiting rooms, hot and crowded, with some kids crawling on the floor and others playing with communal toys coated with every variety of bacteria and virus known to humanity. I grew increasingly anxious as three o'clock neared.

Finally, at ten minutes to three, I approached the receptionist's desk again. "Listen," I said, unable to keep the irritation I felt out of my voice, "I need to leave now. You'll have to give the doctor a message."

"Oh, okay," she said. I got the vacant stare again. I wasn't sure she even remembered seeing me twenty minutes earlier.

"Now write this down," I said. She looked up at me, surprised by the sharpness of my tone. "Tell Dr. Durkin to call Alison Ross about Kay Boyer's murder. Tell him I want to talk to him before I go to the police." I gave her my phone number. "And tell him it's urgent. He has to call me today, or it'll be too late. Have you got that?" She nodded. I glanced quickly at the note she'd written, and as far as I could tell, she'd jotted down the important stuff. "Thank you," I added graciously and walked out.

When I got to the nursery school, Lindsay was in the playground, blissfully hanging upside down from the old tire that served as a makeshift swing. I'd seen her race other kids to get to that swing first.

While she was happily perched on the swing, I glanced around the playground and glimpsed Joanne Persky. Joanne was the youngest member of the nursery school staff. Early 20s, I guessed. The rest of the staff had to be at least 40.

Joanne's auburn hair shone brightly in the sun. She was wearing a miniskirt in a multicolored fabric, with bright purple tights and a chartreuse turtleneck top completing her outfit. In her brilliant plumage, she stood out against the drab brown leaves covering the playground.

I walked over to say hello. She looked up and smiled. Without any jacket in the cool autumn breeze, she was clutching her arms for warmth, but her smile seemed genuine.

"How's it going, Joanne?" I said. "You're not usually here on Mondays."

"I'm filling in. We're shorthanded with Kay gone," she said.

I nodded. "I should have known." I looked around for Lindsay. She'd landed in the sandbox and was busily scooping sand into a bucket.

"What do you think about Kay's murder, Joanne? Do you think Jack Hines did it?"

Joanne looked down at her sneakers and pushed some of the leaves around with her right foot. "I don't know," she said. "Maybe."

"Did you ever have any contact with him?"

Joanne hesitated. "I'd rather not say," she said, still looking down at her feet, pushing the leaves around some more.

I was startled by her response. Why didn't she want to talk about Jack Hines?

"I just talked to him the other day," I said. "He told me he's innocent."

"Innocent?" Joanne said. "He's not exactly the innocent type."

"What do you mean?"

"Look, I'd rather not talk about him right now," she said, looking into my eyes this time.

"Well, I told him I'd try to find out who really did it. Do you think that was a mistake?"

"That's for you to decide. All I can say is that he's...he's the kind of guy who will try to get away with...with stuff."

Stuff? "What kind of stuff?"

"Mrs. Ross, I don't know you very well, and I probably shouldn't be telling you this, but if you swear you won't tell Rella Cox and the rest of them...."

"I swear I won't, Joanne."

"Okay. Well, Jack's a pretty good-looking guy, don't you think?"

I nodded.

"The first time I talked to him, it was kind of late in the afternoon, a couple months ago," Joanne said. "Everyone else had left for the day. We started talking, and he asked me to have a beer with him. I knew he was a little rough around the edges, but he seemed like, well, like okay. So I said yes, and we went to a bar on Howard Street. I had a few beers, and pretty soon he started looking better and better."

I nodded again. I had an idea where this was going, and I hoped Joanne would keep talking.

She did. "He started telling me how beautiful I was–all that crap–and after a while, after he literally begged me, I let him come back to my place. Talk about stupid!"

"Why stupid?"

Joanne paused before answering. "You're a married woman with a nice husband, right? You probably don't remember what it's like to be single. A guy comes onto you, and...sometimes you make a stupid decision. Like I did with Jack."

"Was he abusive? Did he hurt you?" Maybe Jack had revealed a streak of violence I needed to know about.

"He was a little rough, yeah. But that's not unusual with guys like him." Joanne clearly had encountered other men like Jack. "That wasn't the worst part."

"What was?"

"I saw him a couple more times. He never said a word about...about anything. Then, a little while later, I started getting some...some symptoms. Down there." Joanne gestured toward her crotch with her chin. She looked away for a second, then looked back at me. Her mouth had tightened into a grimace. "My doctor, she told me that miserable bastard gave me the clap!"

"How awful," I rushed to say. I'd never known anyone who told me she had gonorrhea or anything like it, but it had to be distinctly unpleasant.

"She gave me an antibiotic, and I was okay pretty fast. But I never want to have anything to do with that bastard again."

I nodded.

"Not that he didn't keep asking...," she said. "But I've steered clear of that guy ever since. And if I were you, I wouldn't believe a word he said."

"Thanks for telling me, Joanne," I said. I knew it must have been hard for her to tell me something so private.

Unexpectedly, I now had something new to think about. Jack Hines was a pretty distasteful character after all.

But sexual misconduct wasn't in the same category as murder, was it? True, he hadn't told Joanne he had the clap, but young men aren't always looking after the best interests of their sexual partners. Murder was something else again.

Just then Lindsay ran over to me, coated from head to toe with sand. I said goodbye to Joanne, brushed Lindsay off, put her in the car, and headed for home.

Missy arrived home about the same time we did, and I was busy playing "Candyland" and "Chutes and Ladders" with the girls for the rest of the afternoon. I almost forgot I was expecting a call from Frank Durkin. But at 5:30, just after Marv got home and we began fixing dinner, the phone rang. Missy ran for it. A moment later she announced, "It's for you, Mommy."

I went upstairs to use the bedroom phone so I could talk without first-floor noise in the background. "Hello?" I said.

"This is Dr. Durkin. I got a rather strange message from you today." His voice had an undertone of anger.

"I'm sorry I had to leave a message like that. I just didn't know any other way to get through to you."

"Well, Linda was quite shocked by it," he said. Funny, Linda didn't seem like someone who shocked easily. "You didn't have to be so explicit, did you?"

"I think I did," I said. "Would you have called me now if I hadn't been?"

There was a long pause. Finally he said, "What's this about anyway? My time is valuable; I have a dozen other calls to make."

"It's about Kay Boyer," I said. "I have reason to believe that you and she had a...a very close relationship, and you broke it off the day before she died."

"That's utter nonsense!" he snapped.

"Is it?"

Another long pause. I decided to fill the vacuum.

"As you probably know, the police are investigating Kay's murder, and I think they should know about you and Kay."

"Even if you're right about me and Kay–and I'm not saying you are–why should the police know? They've already arrested someone."

"Because I'm not sure the man they arrested killed her."

I waited a long time for him to speak again.

"Listen, I don't know anything about you, but if you're trying to get some money out of me, you're making a big mistake."

"I don't want any money, Dr. Durkin. I just want to talk to you."

"Why?"

"Because someone needs to know what happened between you and Kay."

"What the hell? Why in God's name is this any business of yours?"

"Look, the police arrested Jack Hines for the murder because I saw him at the nursery school just before I found Kay's body. So I feel responsible for his arrest. And it seems there was a lot going on in Kay Boyer's life that the police don't know about. I'm just trying to make sure they arrested the right person."

Silence.

"Maybe it would be better if I met you somewhere," I said. "A phone call isn't...."

"I'm a very busy man," he interrupted. "I don't have time for this nonsense. My wife is expecting me home for dinner, and I have to get through a lot of phone calls first."

I had to come up with something fast. "Why don't I meet you for a quick drink somewhere? You can get through your calls and meet me on your way home," I said. "It won't take long. Just call your wife and tell her you'll be a few minutes later than usual. I'm sure she'll understand."

I'll bet she will, I thought. Frank Durkin had no doubt been late for dinner many times before.

Durkin hesitated.

"It won't take long," I repeated.

"All right," he said grudgingly. "But don't expect me to have more than one fast drink with you."

"Okay."

"Where shall I meet you?"

"Umm..., let me think," I said. Where could we meet for a drink? East Winnette didn't have any bars; most suburbs on the North Shore didn't. It would have to be a restaurant with a bar.

I remembered a place where Marv and I once had drinks at a cozy little bar before dinner. "How about Marlee's? Marlee's Restaurant in Evanston?" I asked.

"I know where it is. I'll be there in an hour."

"Fine." I hung up, then ran downstairs to tell Marv.

CHAPTER 22

We got through dinner quickly. Marv didn't look happy when I told him I was meeting Frank Durkin at Marlee's. But after I explained about Thelma Eisenmayer, he understood why I needed to do it. "Take care, sweetness," he said as I kissed him and the girls goodbye and ran out the back door.

It was cold and dark outside, and I was suddenly sorry I'd suggested Marlee's. Parking in Evanston would be a bitch again, and I envisioned having to walk a distance from my car in the dark. But I was lucky and found a parking spot pretty close to Marlee's.

I must be doing something right, I thought. At least the parking gods were looking out for me.

I took a seat at the bar and looked around. It suddenly occurred to me that I had no idea what Frank Durkin looked like. Unlike my rendezvous with Thelma Eisenmayer in Sheridan Park that afternoon, I had no identifying features like a blue Chevy with which to recognize him.

I'll just have to wait and see who tries to pick me up, I thought. I ordered a glass of white wine and waited.

A number of men straggled into the bar, but none of them looked like a pediatrician who'd been married for 35 years. Most were young business executives carrying attaché cases. A few looked like bearded professorial types from nearby Northwestern University. Finally a cleanshaven older man walked in.

He was sixtyish and medium height with bushy eyebrows and a full head of salt-and-pepper hair. His trim-fitting navy blue suit looked pretty sharp—more fashionable than the attire of most of the doctors I knew. He was glancing around the bar, and his otherwise attractive face looked agitated.

I called out, "Dr. Durkin?"

He walked over to me right away. "Mrs. Ross?"

"Yes," I answered. "Please call me Alison."

"Frank."

"Okay," I said, "Frank." He ordered a scotch on the rocks, then turned toward me.

"Now just what is it you want to know? You seem to know a lot already."

"Well…. I've learned that you and Kay Boyer had a relationship, an intimate relationship, but you were trying to break it off just before she was killed."

"Who told you that?"

"I'm sorry, I can't tell you." I prayed he wouldn't realize Thelma had contacted me.

He looked away, then at me. "And you think I killed her."

"I…I didn't say that," I said quickly. "I just wanted to ask you some questions." I took a sip of my wine and tried to calm down.

Frank pulled out a pack of cigarettes and lit one. A stupid choice for a doctor, I thought. But I knew a lot of doctors were still ignoring the advice of the Surgeon General, as well as their own medical knowledge, and continued to smoke.

"Look, Alison, I really don't know why I'm here. I don't even know why I agreed to meet you. But you seem like a nice young woman, and I'll tell you what happened so you can go back home to your family and forget about all of this."

His tone was just a little too patronizing. Was this how he talked to his patients' mothers? If it was, I was glad I'd never switched from Charlotte Henry.

"Kay Boyer and I had, as you put it, an intimate relationship," he said. "I won't deny it. She practically threw herself at me in the beginning, and she was damned attractive, so I had no objections. We had a pretty good thing going for a while, too," he mused, his eyes glazing over as he recalled the beginning of their relationship. "Kay knew how to please a man, and she liked me to please her, too. She wasn't getting any romance out of that old goat of a husband, and she was pretty eager. We had some great times."

I could hardly believe Frank's willingness to tell me the intimate details of their relationship. I felt my face begin to flush. Luckily, in the bar's dim light he probably wouldn't notice.

"We met at first at the nursery school," he continued. "What a kick that was! Doing it in Kay's office, just down the hall from the room where she'd cut out little horsies and kitties with the kids an hour before. There was a certain excitement about it...." An illicit smile crossed his face. "But Kay got nervous. She was afraid someone would walk in on us. So we started going to the Evanston Inn, a block or two from this place."

Why was he so eager to talk about his affair with Kay? Was he egotistical enough to view it as a notch in his bow? "Did anyone ever see you together?" I asked.

"I don't think so. We'd drive over here in separate cars and go into the motel separately," he said. "And things went smashingly for a long time." He almost smirked as he said it.

He finished his scotch and ordered another one. He wasn't in a hurry to get home after all.

"What happened?" I asked.

"What happened?" he repeated. Frank took one last drag on his cigarette and extinguished it in the ashtray on our table. "What do you mean?"

"Didn't things start to go wrong between you?" I asked. "Didn't you try to break up with Kay last week?"

"Things went bad long before last week," he said. "A few months ago Kay started talking about marriage. She wanted to get a divorce, and she figured I did, too. If we both got divorced, she said, we could get married to each other."

"And?"

"And I said 'no.' I didn't want any part of it. The sex was fine, but marriage? Absolutely not!"

"Why not?" I asked.

"Look, I already have a perfectly good marriage. My wife knows I sleep around, and she doesn't care. She's there for me when I want her, and she doesn't bother me when I don't. She takes care of the house and keeps me in touch with our kids, and I'm happy with things the way they are." Sounds like a great marriage, I thought. "Besides, a divorce would be a disaster for me financially."

Of course. The financial angle always loomed large. "But what about Kay?" I asked. "Surely she meant more to you than a cheap affair." He didn't answer. "Didn't she?"

He paused while he lit another cigarette. "Not really," he said finally. "I had no objection to a little sex in the afternoon now and then, even though it screwed up my schedule every time I left the office. But marriage was a whole different ball game. I thought Kay and I had an understanding. It was supposed to be sex and nothing more. Could I help it if she suddenly got serious and I didn't?"

"So you decided to dump her."

"Of course I did," Frank said. "I told her marriage was out, but she kept nagging me about it, threatening to leave me. Finally I told her, 'Fine, leave me. I can always find someone else.' I'd met Linda by that time anyway."

"Linda? Your receptionist?"

He nodded, taking another sip of his scotch.

"She's your new...new...?" I stammered. Had he lied to Thelma Eisenmayer when he told her he was replacing her with his cousin?

"Pretty hot number, isn't she?" Frank was definitely smirking now. In the time it took him to drink two scotches, he'd turned from a reasonably respectable man of 60 into a lecherous womanizer. I took another gulp of wine.

"What did Kay do when you told her you wanted to split up?"

"She wasn't happy about it. Where was she going to find another guy like me?" He smiled a cocky smile. Then it faded. "Frankly, she was pretty upset. She wanted to leave her husband, but I got the feeling she was scared to go it alone. I think she saw me as a way out of her miserable home life, and when I said goodbye, she didn't know exactly what to do."

"Did she...did she threaten you in any way?" I tried to sound vague about Kay's threats. I didn't want to endanger Thelma Eisenmayer.

"Threaten me?" Frank looked indignant. "Of course not. What could she possibly threaten me with?"

"Telling your wife, maybe?"

"Oh, Barbara knows all about my affairs. A threat like that would be meaningless." Frank ordered another scotch.

"Did she...did she threaten to tell anyone else? Like...like the parents of your patients?"

"What?" Frank's brown eyes opened wide. "Whatever gave you that idea?"

"Well, I just...it just occurred to me that she might have said something like that—if she was really angry with you."

He looked at me carefully before responding. "She never suggested doing that," he said finally. "She was furious with me, of course, but she had a reputation in the community to maintain. She never would have told anyone about us." He put out his cigarette, downed his third scotch, and got up to leave.

"Please stay another minute," I said. There were still some unanswered questions.

"Sorry. I need to get home. But...." He seemed to remember something. "There's something I wanted to ask *you*."

"Me?"

"When exactly was Kay killed?" he asked.

"You mean the time of death?"

"Yes."

"The medical examiner said it was about eight or eight-thirty that morning."

A smug smile crept over Frank's face. "If you've been harboring any suspicion that I murdered Kay, you can forget it. I was on my rounds at the hospital at eight o'clock last Tuesday."

"The hospital?"

"Doctors' Hospital, here in Evanston." Frank said. "I'm there several mornings a week to see patients."

"And you were there at eight o'clock Tuesday morning?"

"That's right," he said. "From quarter to eight till nine-thirty." The smile lingered on his face.

I nodded, wondering if the hospital kept records of its doctors' rounds.

"Well, it's been lovely, Alison," he said. Was I imagining it, or was he leering suggestively at *me* now? His smile had become a glittery-eyed leer, I was sure of it. "But I really must be going."

"Thanks for your time, Frank. I really appreciate it," I said. I watched him as he strode out of the bar.

What had actually happened between him and Kay Boyer? Thelma Eisenmayer had no reason to lie, did she? She'd heard Kay threaten to expose Frank Durkin. Or had she? Frank had just denied to me that she did.

I remembered hearing that doctors are always likely murder suspects because they have both the knowledge and the nerve to commit murder. Had Frank Durkin killed Kay Boyer? He certainly had the knowledge, and he appeared to have more than enough nerve.

If Kay had threatened to expose his amorous adventures to the community, potentially damaging his reputation, and by extension his successful practice, he had a motive, too. He was familiar with the layout of the nursery school, and he must have known that Kay Boyer frequently arrived at eight o'clock in the morning.

Even if he'd really been on his rounds at the hospital Tuesday morning, Doctors' Hospital was no more than ten or fifteen minutes away from the nursery school. Frank could have left the hospital, driven to the nursery school, and returned to the hospital without anyone's noticing his absence.

I left Marlee's, wondering as I drove home whether Frank Durkin had murdered Kay Boyer.

CHAPTER 23

I didn't sleep well Monday night. Everything Frank Durkin and Thelma Eisenmayer told me whirled around in my head. I couldn't forget Joanne Persky's revelations either. I kept trying to sort it all out.

Tuesday morning I awoke tired and irritable. When Marv and Missy left for school, I couldn't help thinking it was exactly one week ago that I'd found Kay Boyer's body. A week had passed, and I was more confused about her murder than ever.

Somehow I got through the morning at home with Lindsay. When she went upstairs to play some records, I began doing mindless household chores that I usually avoid. I welcomed them now as a way to keep busy while thoughts about the murder dominated my consciousness. At one point I tried phoning Charlotte Henry, but her answering service said she was at a medical convention and wouldn't be back till next week.

I was making lunch for Lindsay when the phone rang.

"Alison?" A male voice. Familiar, but I couldn't pin it down. "This is Neal. Neal Bannister."

"Oh, Neal. How are you?" My pulse rate perked up as I pictured his Paul Newman-like looks.

"Great, Alison. Listen, I only have a minute. I've got some information on Kidd's Korner for you."

"You do? Fantastic! What is it?"

"Can't tell you right now. Got an important lunch meeting with some customers. Can we get together later?"

"Sure. When?"

"How's eight o'clock?"

"Eight o'clock? Tonight?"

"I'm afraid so. I'm tied up all afternoon. Can you meet me at my office at eight? I have something to show you."

"Well...," I hesitated. I wasn't ready to tell Marv I was meeting Neal, even though our connection was perfectly innocent. Meeting Neal alone in his office wasn't precisely like meeting Frank Durkin at a public place like Marlee's. Marv might object....

Neal broke in. "It should only take a few minutes. My office is here in East Winnette, in that new office building next to Walgreen's."

Next door to Walgreen's, five minutes from my house. I could tell Marv I needed something at the drug store. "Okay, Neal. I think I can make it."

"Great, Alison. See you then." He hung up.

I looked at my watch. I had only fifteen minutes to get Lindsay fed and off to school. I rushed her through lunch, raced to school, and returned home. Thinking about Neal's call, I remembered that I'd tried to call Bree Boyer the day before, just before I heard from Thelma Eisenmayer. I tried calling Bree at home again. Still no answer.

What about trying to get some background information on Frank Durkin? I grabbed a phone book and looked him up. His only listing was the medical office in downtown East Winnette. But a B. Durkin was listed at 225 Forest Drive.

Frank had referred to his wife as "Barbara" when we talked at Marlee's. Didn't Jerry, my doctor-cousin, avoid nuisance calls by listing his home phone and address under his wife's name?

Frank Durkin was probably using the same dodge. Maybe this was the sort of tip doctors gave each other at medical conventions.

I wondered about Barbara Durkin. What was she like? Frank had said his wife knew about his love affairs and didn't care, but what kind of woman knew all about her husband's infidelities and didn't care?

Maybe Frank had lied to me. Maybe his wife really didn't know. Maybe he'd managed to keep his extracurricular romances a secret until Kay Boyer came along.

What if Kay paid Barbara Durkin a visit, right after she left Frank's office that Monday afternoon? Barbara might have exploded when she heard what Kay had to say. Maybe she'd confronted Frank that night, and he–or she–had turned up at the nursery school the next morning, ready to do battle with Kay.

What did Barbara know—about Frank's affairs in general, and about Kay Boyer in particular? Maybe I could get her to talk to me. It was worth a try.

I phoned B. Durkin's number, but no one answered. Maybe she was home but, for some reason, couldn't come to the phone. 225 Forest Drive was only a few blocks away, maybe two minutes from my house by car. I decided to check out the Durkin home.

But I wouldn't drive. I'd walk. It was another beautiful crisp fall day, and I needed the exercise. I loved walking around East Winnette anyway. No two houses in East Winnette, built at different times, even different centuries, were exactly the same. I liked to look at their exteriors and try to imagine how they looked inside.

I walked briskly and got to 225 Forest in less than ten minutes. The house, sitting on a big lot about a block from the

lake, was enormous. With an ugly brown brick exterior, nothing like Andrea Lewis's mansion, it made me salivate just the
same. I could tell it was the kind of old house I longed for: five
or six high-ceilinged rooms on the first floor, fireplaces everywhere, a huge second floor with maybe four or five bedrooms. I
ached just to look at it.

Doctors complained a lot—about malpractice suits, the
high cost of insurance, and the pressures of dealing with difficult patients. But despite their complaints, they seemed to
live in pretty high style.

I climbed the front steps and rang the doorbell. No one
answered. I tried leaning over the handrail to look inside the
living room window, but I couldn't get close enough to see
anything.

I made my way down the steps and onto the front lawn.
Maybe I could see something through the windows. But carefully trimmed evergreen bushes were in the way.

Okay, maybe Barbara Durkin was in her back yard. She
might be gardening or merely sunning herself. I walked
around the side of the house on a flagstone path. But instead of
the large grassy yard I expected to find, a big rectangular swim-
ming pool took up most of the space between the house and the
detached garage.

The pool looked as though no one had swum in it for
weeks. The water was covered with dead leaves that moved
slowly in the breeze coming off the lake. No one appeared to
be around.

I turned to look back at the house. The Durkins had
clearly done some remodeling. Remodeling old houses was a
passion in East Winnette. Each summer every block had at
least one major renovation project going on.

The Durkins had apparently added a large family room at the back of the house. Sliding glass doors led from the new family room to a well-designed patio adjacent to the pool. You'd never know from looking at the front of the house that a pricey up-to-date addition existed in the back. A lot of houses on the North Shore could fool you that way.

People didn't seem to need "family rooms" years ago when these old houses were built. But by this time, most of the houses on our block had added a family room, where our neighbors stashed their TVs and phonographs, their board games and kids' toys, instead of cluttering up their fancy living rooms.

We still didn't have a family room. I liked to tell people we were preserving a venerable tradition by actually "living" in our living room. The truth was we'd have loved to have a family room in the back of our house, but so far we hadn't scraped up enough cash to add one on.

It occurred to me that Barbara Durkin might be in her family room. Maybe she'd gone there to read or watch TV and had dozed off. Or maybe she was in the bathroom when I rang the bell. It wouldn't hurt to glance inside through the glass doors.

I walked through the patio, skirting the white umbrella table and matching chairs, and approached the glass doors. The room appeared to be deserted. I knocked on the glass, thinking someone might hear me. Silence.

I tried moving the handle of the glass door, and surprisingly, the door began to slide. I could barely believe it: the door wasn't locked. I slid the door open, far enough for me to enter the house.

Now that I was inside, I didn't know exactly what to do. I was still in a mild state of shock. It always amazed me that some people on the North Shore actually left their doors unlocked. I could never walk to the corner without securely locking both my front and back doors. I got anxiety attacks just thinking about strangers entering my house, even when no one was home.

I looked around the Durkins' family room. It was stylishly decorated with white rattan furniture and custom-made cushions in a fresh-looking flower print full of lime green and yellow and bright blue. I didn't know Barbara Durkin, but I sure admired her taste.

I wondered what to do next. Should I look for Barbara, or should I look for something else? Something connecting Frank Durkin to Kay Boyer?

The family room was clearly not the place to find either Barbara or any incriminating evidence, so I walked toward the front of the house, hoping I would get some idea of what to look for. I passed through a spotless kitchen, its decor coordinated with the family room's. It looked recently remodeled, complete with top-of-the-line appliances ordered through one of those custom kitchen places.

I kept going, through an elegantly furnished dining room with a large bay window, then into a hallway that presumably led to the living room. But just off the hallway I noticed a small room, one of those intriguing nooks and crannies the old houses on the North Shore had in spades.

The small room appeared to be a study, filled with a teak desk, matching teak bookcases, a comfortable leather reclining chair, and a metal filing cabinet. Frank Durkin's study?

I entered and began to look around. The walls were covered with Norman Rockwell reproductions of doctors in assorted sentimental poses, along with several diplomas and certificates attesting to the professional competence of one Frank Durkin, M.D. It suddenly hit me that I was in Frank's study without his permission. But this was my chance to try to find something.

I approached the desk. The top was nearly bare, with only an onyx pen-and-pencil set, engraved with Frank's name and the phrase "with everlasting gratitude," front and center. Probably a gift from the grateful parents of a child who'd overcome a dreaded disease with Frank's assistance.

Did the desk drawers hold something incriminating? I boldly opened the top drawer. Nothing but pens, pencils, a prescription pad, and other writing supplies.

The second drawer was a lot messier. It held miscellaneous receipts and some odd bits of paper with phone numbers and other notes on them. Stuck in the back was a small brown address book with a well-worn leather cover. I pulled it out and opened it to the page headed "B."

I didn't see the name "Boyer," but "KB" was written in pencil halfway down the page. The phone number was an East Winnette number, and it seemed familiar. Maybe it was the nursery school's.

I looked quickly through the rest of the address book, but none of the other names meant anything to me. I wondered whether I should take the book with me. If the number listed for "KB" was the nursery school, the book was evidence that Frank knew Kay Boyer and phoned her there.

Not much, but it was something.

I hesitated. What if Frank looked for the book and found it missing?

He'd never know who took it. He'd probably assume he misplaced it. I slipped it into my purse.

I searched the other desk drawers but couldn't find anything else. What was I hoping to find? A letter, a photograph? The drawers were void of anything like that.

I turned toward the filing cabinet and opened the top drawer. A dozen file folders filled the drawer, identified with phrases like "Paper, Rockford Conference 1978" and "X-rays 1976." Nothing useful.

The second file drawer contained another batch of folders. Again, nothing looked promising—except one, buried in the back. It looked different, older than the other folders. "California" was printed on it in faded black ink. I pulled it out and opened it.

A single piece of paper fell out of the folder. I picked it up. It was a legal document, an "order to show cause" issued by the medical licensing board in California, dated June 10, 1967. Something about showing cause why the license of Frank Durkin, M.D., should not be suspended.

The folder was otherwise empty. Impulsively, I folded the yellowing document and stuck it inside my purse, next to the address book, and replaced the folder in the drawer.

I glanced at my watch. Nearly 1:15. Someone might be coming home, and I didn't want to be prowling through the house if that happened. I walked back into the hallway and headed toward the family room and the sliding glass doors.

As I passed through the glass doors onto the patio, I heard a car door slam inside the garage. I stood frozen in my tracks, then decided to make a run for it around the side of the house. But before I could thread my way through the patio furniture, a woman emerged from the garage. I felt her eyes on me as I tried to keep walking.

"Just a minute there!" she called out. "Who are you?" I didn't say anything. "What are you doing here?" Her tone was indignant, but there was an undertone of fear as well.

I stopped and turned to look at her as she warily approached me. Squinting to see her better in the bright sunlight, I noted that she was middle-aged, on the short side, and slightly over-weight. Her hair, styled *à la mode*, was an unnaturally youth-ful red. In her chic and undoubtedly expensive beige suit, her plump figure appeared almost trim.

"Well? Who are you, and what are you doing here?" she repeated.

I was speechless. It had to be Barbara Durkin, but my idea of talking to her, of trying to find out what she knew about her husband and Kay Boyer, now seemed idiotic. My mind raced as I tried to think of something to say.

Sunlight reflecting on the water in the pool caught my eye.

Dead leaves moved slowly in the water.

I said the first thing that popped into my mind. "I'm...I'm from a pool-cleaning service. We're contacting peo-ple about getting their pools cleaned before the bad weather starts."

Barbara's eyes narrowed. She was trying to decide whether I was telling the truth. "We have someone coming to clean the pool later this afternoon," she said finally. "You're not from Pool-ish People, are you?"

"Pool-ish People? No, no, I'm not."

"Well, who *do* you represent?" she asked suspiciously.

"Uh...the...uh...." She was still looking at me through half-closed eyes. "East Winnette Pools," I blurted out.

"East Winnette Pools? I've never heard of it."

"We're a new company," I said quickly. "That's why you've never heard of us. That's why we're going door-to-door." I tried to reassure her with a saleswomanly smile. "We need to let people know we're looking for business."

She hesitated. "I see. Well, why don't you give me your card? I'll call you for an estimate next time."

Say something, Alison. Anything. "Oh, I'm sorry, ma'am. "I'm fresh out of cards. Just gave the last one to a woman up the block."

"Where was that? This is the only pool on this block." She began to look suspicious again.

"Uh...the woman I talked to, she said they're thinking of putting in a pool. I don't remember which house it was, ma'am."

"Hmm...," she said. "Well then, come back another time." She turned and headed toward the sliding glass doors.

"It was nice talking to you, ma'am. Goodbye now," I called out as I sped through the patio and around the side of the house.

When I got to the corner of Forest Drive and Second Street, my heart was pounding. I stopped and took a deep breath.

What had I gotten myself into?

CHAPTER 24

I strode home quickly, surprised that I could walk so fast when I felt so shaky. I wanted to forget the whole miserable mess. Drop it right there and leave it to the police. I could return the money to Elmira Hines and simply tell her to find someone else.

I poured myself a Diet Pepsi and sank into the living room sofa, trying to relax. Just forget the whole thing, Alison. You don't have the skills to do this job right. Call Bob Shakespear. Let him take it from here. Let him talk to Frank Durkin, let him question Bree Boyer.

Bree Boyer....

Wait a minute, Alison. You forgot about Bree Boyer.

No, I wouldn't turn it over to Bob Shakespear, not yet. I wanted to talk to Bree first. I had the feeling she was hiding something. Something that was eating away at her.

I was pretty sure the police hadn't succeeded at getting Bree to say very much. And even if Bob Shakespear approached her again, he might never get her to reveal what she was hiding.

Maybe if I could talk to her for a few minutes...alone... maybe she'd trust me, someone who knew and admired her mother. Trust me enough to reveal what was eating away at her.

I picked up the phone and dialed Bree's number. The phone rang for a long time. I stayed on the line until finally a weak voice answered.

"Bree?"

"Who's this?" Her voice was so weak I could barely hear it.

"Bree, it's Alison Ross. You don't sound very good." I paused, but she didn't respond. "Are you all right?"

"I'm okay," she said unconvincingly. "Why are you calling me again?"

"I'd like to come by to see you. You don't sound okay. Maybe I can help."

"Look, I took a sleeping pill in the middle of the night. I haven't slept it off yet."

"You still...."

"What time is it?"

"About 1:30."

She sighed. "Damn, I missed my class again."

"Please, Bree, I'd like to come over. To check that you're all right."

"Okay, okay," she said resignedly. "I'll be here." She hung up.

I drove to the old white-frame house one more time. I climbed the crumbling concrete steps and rang the bell. After a long wait, Bree opened the door, dressed in a worn green flannel robe.

"Come in," she said, pushing her brown curls away from her face. Her voice seemed stronger. The sleeping pill had begun to wear off.

I entered the dark living room and seated myself on the sofa. Bree sat down in a threadbare chair facing me. "Well, what is it?" she asked.

"Do you know why I'm here?"

"Not really."

"I think you do."

"I do?" She twisted her mouth into a sardonic scowl. "Remind me."

"I think you're trying to hide something, Bree. I think you know something about your mother's murder that you haven't told anyone." She didn't respond. "Am I right?"

"You sure don't stop trying, do you?" Bree asked. "What business is it of yours anyway?"

"Someone–someone who may be innocent–has been charged with your mother's murder. Do you want to see him convicted for something he didn't do?"

Bree hesitated. "Okay, okay, maybe you're right. Maybe he didn't do it. But why do you think I know anything about it?"

"I'm not sure, Bree. But something tells me you do."

Bree looked away. She rose from her chair, walked to the window, and stared out at the street.

I walked over to her. Impulsively, I put my hand on her arm. "I want to help, Bree. I want to help you–and the rest of your family. Please believe me."

She shrugged off my hand and turned to look at me. "But all your snooping isn't going to help us. Don't you see that?" She walked away from me, heading toward the back of the house. I followed her.

Bree stopped when she got to the kitchen, where cheerless brown-and-beige wallpaper bordered dark wooden cabinets. A large wooden table, surrounded by six chairs, sat in the middle of the room.

I tried to picture the Boyer family seated around the table, eating dinner together, laughing and talking.

I couldn't picture it.

Bree poured herself a Coke. "Want one?" she offered. I nodded. Bree poured another Coke and handed it to me.

"So you want to help our family," she said, an ironic smile flickering across her face. "And you think all these questions are going to help us. What a joke!"

"Why do you say that?"

"Because you don't know a thing about this family!" she erupted. Her bitterness, her hate, for something or someone, was beginning to surface.

"What do you mean?" I felt awkward standing next to the table. I pulled out one of the chairs and sat down.

"This is one very sick family, Alison. I don't think you have any idea just how sick it is." Bree began to pace around the kitchen. "Everyone at the nursery school thought my mother was so wonderful. So marvelous with kids, so marvelous with their parents. Everyone just worshipped her. Well, my mother...my mother...."

Bree slammed her Coke down on the table. She put her face into her outstretched palms and began to cry.

"Your mother *was* a wonderful woman," I said, jumping up and going over to Bree. I put my hand on her shoulder this time. She shrugged it off.

"Maybe she didn't spend as much time with you as you wanted, but I'm sure she loved you. She just got caught up with her work, with the school, and...and other things." I thought of Frank Durkin and his trysts with Kay at the Evanston Inn. "It happens to a lot of people. They may focus on their work for a while, but that doesn't mean they don't love...."

"You don't have any idea what went on in this house!" Bree broke in. "Don't tell me about my mother. It was because of that school that she was never home, and he...he...."

"He?"

"My father." She spat out the words.

"Your father? What about your father?" I had totally forgotten about Tom Boyer. That feeble, depressing old man. Bree began to cry again. "What about him, Bree? Please tell me."

Bree stopped crying. She sniffed back her tears and straightened her shoulders. She seemed to have reached some sort of decision.

"Okay, okay" she said, "I'll tell you. I'll tell you something I've never told anyone before, except...except my mother." She briefly flashed her ironic smile.

"I'll start with Julie. Did you know I had a sister named Julie?" I nodded. "She was seven years older than me," Bree began, finally seating herself at the table.

I sat down next to her and looked into her face. Her deep blue eyes were staring into mine. "Because of the age difference, we weren't close, but I always looked up to her. When I was a little girl, I thought she was the smartest, the most beautiful, the most wonderful girl in the world. I wanted to be just like her.

"But once I got a little older, I realized there was something wrong. She'd be happy one minute, fooling around with Wes and me, and then all of a sudden, she'd change. She'd start to look really sad, as though she could hardly bear what the world held in store for her."

Something like the way you look right now, Bree.

"I'd try to make her laugh, or smile. I'd try to get her to play games or watch TV with me. And sometimes she would. But she spent a lot of time alone, up in her room, and I couldn't get her to do things with me. She had a few girlfriends she'd see sometimes. But she was pretty much of a loner, most of the time up in her room, reading or playing records."

I didn't know where this was going, but I kept nodding, hoping Bree's description of her sister was leading somewhere.

"One day, about ten years ago," she went on, "when I was 11 and Julie was 18, I came home from school, and the house was quiet. Wes wasn't living at home anymore, and of course my mother wasn't there. My father was gone, too. God knows where he was.

"I ran upstairs to look for Julie. She was going to junior college in Glenview Park by then, and she always got home from school before I did. But it was real quiet in the house, like no one was there. I opened Julie's door, and...and that's when I saw her."

Bree looked down at her hands, then back at me. "She was dead." Bree's blue eyes had an icy glazed stare. "I didn't know it at first. She had a rope—the clothesline from the basement—around her neck. She must have climbed up on a chair, tied the rope to the light fixture on the ceiling, and...and kicked the chair away."

My heart started to pound as Bree went on. "I was paralyzed at first. I didn't know what to do. Finally I...I ran out of the room and called Mom to come home from school right away. I couldn't go back in that room. Julie's face was...distorted, ugly. I didn't want to remember her that way."

"Of course not," I said.

What a terrifying discovery. Her older sister, someone she loved, hanging from a clothesline. I shuddered just to think about it.

"Later I found a note in my room," Bree continued.

"A note?"

"Julie had left me a note. In my underwear drawer. She knew I'd find it there."

"And...?"

"It said, 'I want to die because of Daddy. He made my life a nightmare. Don't let him do it to you.'"

Bree looked away from me for a moment. Then her eyes came back to mine. "I didn't understand the note at all. Not then. Julie and my father always seemed to get along great. He paid a lot of attention to her. At least it seemed like a lot, compared to the attention Wes and I got. He was always taking her shopping and out to movies and museums. He'd buy her clothes and jewelry, gifts like that. I was even jealous sometimes."

I began to get a sick feeling in the pit of my stomach. I was certain I knew what Bree was going to say next.

"Pretty soon I began to understand what Julie meant," Bree said. "A few months after she died, Daddy started paying attention to me. He began taking me out to places the way he had with Julie, and buying me little gifts, and telling me how pretty I was. He'd barely noticed me before.

"One afternoon I came home from school, and Daddy was there alone. Mom wasn't due home till dinnertime. Daddy told me he wanted to show me something in his bedroom. I went up there with him. And...." Bree hesitated. "Do I have to tell you the rest?" she asked.

"No," I said. She didn't have to tell me. I knew what had happened to Bree, and to her sister Julie before her. My heart was still pounding, and now I felt nauseated, too. For a moment I thought I might throw up. All over the Boyers' dirty kitchen floor.

"Well, what do you think of our family now, Alison? Not quite your wholesome all-American family, is it?" Bree asked. She had a grim smile on her face.

"No, it wasn't. But...but you said you told your mother. Why didn't she do something about it?"

"I didn't tell Mom anything until....I ended my story too soon, Alison. There's more. Lots more." She took a deep breath.

"I put up with my father's demands for a long time. I know I shouldn't have. I should have gone to someone–my mother, my teachers, anyone who could have helped me. But I didn't."

"Why not?"

"Well, in a way I liked the closeness, the attention I was getting from him. I sensed we were doing something wrong— but I was confused. I didn't really understand what was happening. I guess I wanted the love and attention I got if I let him touch me."

"And your mother...?"

"She wasn't around very much. She'd get home from school late, and she'd be exhausted. By the time she got dinner on the table—my father never cooked–she didn't have much energy left. Some nights she'd go back to the school for meetings or parents' nights, or sometimes she'd go to meetings of the North Shore Teachers' League. If she stayed home, she'd usually go to bed pretty early, and I wouldn't see her again until the morning."

"What about weekends?"

"Weekends she was busy doing errands, getting groceries, going to conferences. I barely had a chance to spend time with her. So I was happy when my father started spending so much time with me.

"He'd give me money and presents and buy me nice clothes. He told me he'd stop doing all that if I told anyone. I liked getting all those nice things, so I went along with it."

Bree got up and began to pace again. Her face had a stricken look. She was clearly still haunted by everything that had happened to her.

I was wondering what I could say to comfort her when she began speaking again. "When I was 13 or 14, I began to get fed up with my father's demands. He wasn't doing anything that hurt me physically. But I didn't like what we were doing, and I told him I didn't want to go to bed with him anymore."

"How did he react?"

"At first he acted like I hadn't said anything. So then I said that if he didn't stop what he was doing, I'd go to Mom and tell her about it."

"And...?"

"I could almost see the gears turning inside his head. He was trying to think of what to say. Finally he said that if I told her, she wouldn't understand. I'd get in trouble. And...and then he said it would kill her if she found out. He said it would kill Mom if I told her or anyone else what we were doing."

Bree paused. "That made a weird kind of sense to me. I was so stupid, so naïve. I was only a kid! I thought he was probably right, that it could kill Mom if she found out. So I didn't tell her. I didn't tell anyone. I loved my mother." She began to cry softly again. "I loved her. Even though...even though she never did anything to help me." Bree's face suddenly showed a hint of anger.

"Don't you think my mother should have helped me, Alison? Couldn't she see what was happening? She should have seen what was happening, she should...."

"But you said you did tell your mother," I interrupted.

"Oh, I'm getting to that." Bree's voice was shaky, but she kept going. "About a year later, I finally told my father it was over. I don't know what gave me the strength to do it. Maybe all the stories about sexual abuse I started hearing on TV. I don't know. But I finally felt strong enough to tell him to leave me alone. I wasn't a child anymore, and something told me I didn't have to put up with him anymore.

"I realized...finally...that everything he'd said to scare me was just a load of bullshit! I wouldn't get in trouble, and it wouldn't kill Mom, if I told her about it. So I told him to leave me alone, or I'd tell my mother. I'd tell the world!" Bree's ironic smile appeared again for a moment. "After that, he left me alone."

"He never touched you again?"

"No. I wouldn't let him get near me. Oh, he begged me to spend those afternoons with him again, but I wouldn't. I didn't want to end up like Julie. That must have been when he turned to those pictures."

"Pictures?"

She nodded. "Pictures of children."

"Pictures of children...? You mean child pornography?"

"Right. After he had a heart attack a few years ago, I went through his drawers looking for clothes to take to the hospital. In the back of one drawer, I found a stash of those pictures. They made me sick. But I guess he got his kicks that way after...after I wouldn't go to bed with him anymore."

I tried to suppress my feelings of revulsion and keep Bree talking. "After you stopped...did you think about going to the police, telling somebody about him?" I asked.

"Oh, no." She shook her head. "I didn't talk about it to anyone. It was too awful, too dirty. I didn't want anyone to know. Besides, by that time I didn't see any reason to tell anyone. Once it was over, once he stopped, what good would it have done? It wouldn't have helped me to tell anyone. Maybe just the opposite. People might have thought I was to blame. I'd gone along with it for so long, who would believe that I didn't want to do it?

"But if you'd...."

"He always said…he always said I liked it. That I wanted it," Bree interrupted. The look of disgust on her face revealed how she really felt. "He might have told people that, even though it was a lie. It's true, I didn't push him away for a long time. I was confused, I trusted him, I liked the attention. But I never wanted the physical part of it.

"Still, I didn't think I could talk to anyone about it. I decided I'd stay in this house till I finished high school and could get my own place. Get away from him. But I wouldn't, I couldn't tell anyone."

"But you said…?"

"Wait a minute. I'm getting to that." She looked annoyed with me. Then the pain returned to her face. "Last Sunday, a week ago Sunday, Wes brought Emily over here. You met Emily, didn't you? Wes's six-year-old daughter?"

I nodded.

"Wes is divorced, and his ex has custody of Emily, but he gets her every other weekend. Well, that Sunday somebody gave him a ticket to the Bears game, and he's a big Bears fan, so he brought Emily over here to stay with us while he went to the game.

"I came here to spend some time with Emily. But about two o'clock I went upstairs to look through some things I'd left in my old bedroom. Emily was in the living room playing a game with my parents.

"About an hour later I decided to join them. I went downstairs, but no one was there. Mom's car was gone. I found out later she'd gone to the Jewel to get some food for dinner. But I didn't know that then. I figured they took Emily out for a walk or something, so I went back upstairs.

"But when I passed my parents' bedroom, I heard some noises. I knocked on the door. I said, 'Mom? Dad?' Then I heard Emily's voice. She yelled, 'Bree!' So I opened the door. My father was in bed...with Emily. He'd taken all her clothes off...."

"That's enough, Bree," I said. "You don't have to tell me any more."

"But you wanted to hear about my mother, didn't you?"

"Yes. Yes, of course." I'd forgotten why I'd come to see Bree in the first place.

"Well, Mom got back a short time later. My father had come up with a ridiculous story about Emily feeling sick, and how he put her to bed so she could get some rest. Incredible! How could he think I'd believe him?" Bree shook her head, amazed that her father expected her, of all people, to believe such a lie.

"I couldn't let my father do this to Emily," she continued. "She's only six! But I didn't know what to do. Should I tell Wes? Tell Mom? Go to the police? I was up all night trying to decide what to do.

"Finally I decided to tell Mom first. She was the expert on children, she went to one conference after another, I figured she had to know what to do. So Monday night I got her alone and told her everything. We talked...we talked for a long time."

Monday night. The night I'd called about Lindsay's stuffed rabbit Tammy. No wonder it took them so long to answer the phone. No wonder they both sounded so distracted when they finally answered.

"I told her everything—about Julie and me and...and about Emily. She was stunned. Absolutely stunned. She said she'd never suspected, never. She said she couldn't even look at my father again, let alone live with him, if it was true. *If it was true....*"

"You mean she didn't believe you?"

"She was so shocked, I don't think she knew what to believe," Bree answered. "But she didn't seem absolutely sure that I was telling the truth. She looked at me funny, almost like she was thinking, 'If it really happened, why did you wait so long to tell me?'"

"So it's possible that she didn't believe you? That she thought you might have encouraged it?"

Bree nodded.

"But you...you were a helpless victim, Bree. You're not to blame for what happened."

Bree nodded. "I wanted Mom to say something like that. I wanted her to say, 'I'm sorry, Bree. I'm sorry that happened to you. I know you weren't to blame.' But she didn't."

I shook my head in disbelief. What was going through Kay's mind when she heard Bree's revelations? Was she really unsure that Bree was telling the truth?

"I guess I'll never know what she was thinking," Bree said. "She seemed in a daze that night anyhow."

Of course she did. And I knew why. Kay had gone to Frank Durkin's office that afternoon and threatened to expose his philandering to his wife, to the parents of his patients. After storming out of his office, she went home, only to face this scene with Bree.

"She finally told me she'd talk to my father later that night. She'd confront him and see what he had to say."

"Was that okay with you?"

"He was her husband. She had to deal with this her own way. But I told her that if he denied it, I'd think about going to the police. And that's how we left it."

"And the next morning...the next morning someone killed her."

Bree nodded her head.

"Do you know...do you know if she actually talked to your father before she was killed?"

"No. I went to bed early that night, right after we finished talking. I hadn't slept the night before. I took a sleeping pill...."

"Bree," I interrupted. "Have you told the police any of this?"

"No," she said, looking away. "When Mom was killed, and the police came to question us, I...I just couldn't tell them. I...." Bree stopped.

"I understand, Bree. I really do." I reached out and lightly touched Bree's hand. She looked back at me. It was clear she didn't think anyone else could possibly understand.

I'd run out of things to say. My head was spinning, and I had to get out of that house to think. "Bree, I'm glad you confided in me. It may...it may help solve your mother's murder." I got up to leave.

"How?" she asked.

"I don't know. I haven't figured that out yet."

She walked back to the living room with me. "Alison," she said, "you know, I'm glad I told you." Her face had brightened a little bit. "I was always afraid to tell people, afraid they'd think I was to blame in some way. But maybe talking about it helps." I nodded.

"I guess I should have talked about it a long time ago. And I probably should have told the police when they questioned me, right after Mom...right after Mom was killed."

"At least you've taken the first step, talking to me," I said. "Now you should talk to someone else, maybe a counselor at your school. And maybe...maybe sometime you'll feel ready to tell the police." I looked at Bree. Her face was impassive, noncommittal.

I shifted my gaze and looked out the living room window. The sky had clouded over, and it looked like rain. "I'd better be going."

"Okay." She walked me to the door.

I said goodbye and waved at her as I walked down the steps. Suddenly I remembered something. I ran back up the steps before she could close the door. "Do you know where your father is now?" I asked.

"No. I've hardly spoken to him since Mom...since Mom died. I've been avoiding him."

"Are you still living here?" I didn't think Bree should be living anywhere near her father if she was going to get her life straightened out.

"I moved out of this house a few years ago. I rent a cheap studio in Rogers Park. I'm just staying here now to sort through Mom's things."

"So you don't know where he is?"

"I think he comes and goes at all hours of the day and night. I guess he's been sleeping here, but I don't know where he goes when he leaves. And I don't care." She closed the door.

I understood, or at least I thought I did. Why should she care about her father? A man like that didn't deserve to get the time of day from the daughter he'd abused.

I left the house and drove off, Bree's story still ringing in my ears.

CHAPTER 25

I'd never heard anyone tell the kind of story Bree had just told me. Oh, I'd read about it in newspapers and magazines, even seen a handful of women on TV who talked about the sordid relationships their fathers had forced on them. But that was nothing like having Bree tell me to my face what had happened to her, a story so ugly she could never put it into words until...until the night she told her mother.

Now I had to wonder what happened when Bree told Kay what her father had done. How did Kay react?

According to Bree, Kay seemed to doubt Bree's story. But she promised Bree she would talk to Tom that night.

Did Kay do what she promised? Did she confront Tom that Monday night?

If she did confront him, how did he respond? Did he deny Bree's story and manage to convince Kay that he was innocent? Or did he admit the truth?

I knew I had to find Tom Boyer, to talk to him myself. But I didn't know where to look. Where did he go when he left his house?

I had a few minutes before pick-up time at the nursery school. I drove over to Sheridan Park and left my car at the beach, near the spot where I'd met Thelma Eisenmayer. Gazing at the lake, I sorted through the events of the past week, the people I'd talked to, the evidence I'd uncovered. But when I left the park for the nursery school, I was nowhere near a solution. I needed to bounce my ideas off someone else.

Back home, I gave Lindsay a snack, handed her some coloring books and crayons, and called Judy from the living room phone. Luckily, she was in her office.

"Do you have a minute to talk? I..."

" Ali," she interrupted, "did you see the latest issue of the alumni bulletin?"

"No...no, Judy, but...."

"You won't believe it. The governor of Montana has appointed Cassie Frick to the Montana Supreme Court."

"Cassie Frick?"

"Yes! It's in the bulletin. Her married name is, let's see... 'Cassandra Frick Benton'. When did she get married?"

"Hmm...a couple of years after she moved to Montana."

"Oh."

I could hear Judy's mind whirring. Maybe a move somewhere like Montana wasn't such a bad idea. Great scenery, wide-open spaces, interesting work...available men.

I remembered that my copy of the alumni bulletin was lying in a forgotten pile of mail somewhere in the dining room. "What else does it say?"

"Nothing else. Just that. So what do you think, Ali? The first person from our class to sit on a state supreme court is Cassie Frick. I can't believe it."

I couldn't either. Cassie and I had been casual friends during law school. She was quiet and kept to herself a lot. Friendly but not very outgoing. I knew she wasn't any smarter than I was.

But now she was on the Montana Supreme Court, and I was...what? Wife, mother, unemployed lawyer...detective?

I was glad I'd decided to keep Elmira Hines's money. At least I could describe myself as a part-time detective.

Suddenly I remembered why I'd called Judy in the first place. "Judy, I need to talk to you. Preferably in person. If I can find someone to watch the girls, can I come downtown and meet you this afternoon?"

"What's up, Ali?"

"It's about my case."

"Your case? You mean the murder?"

"Yep."

"Well, sure. I've got a pile of work on my desk, but I can take a few minutes away from it. Where do you want to meet?"

I vaguely recalled visiting Judy's office once before. "Your firm is in the train-station building, right?"

"Right. Can you meet me at the coffee shop downstairs?"

"If I catch the next train, I can be there in less than an hour."

"Okay. Call me when you get off the train, and I'll meet you downstairs at The Coffee Spot."

I looked out the window and saw Missy approaching our house. Once she was settled inside, snacking and coloring with Lindsay, I rushed back to the phone and called my next-door neighbor, Belinda Coleman.

Belinda was a charming older woman who lived with her second husband in a much grander house than ours. She'd always been warm and friendly towards our little family. She had two grown sons and seemed to take special delight in my young daughters.

Belinda usually stuck pretty close to home, and I prayed she was home right now. Thankfully, she answered the phone after the first ring.

"Belinda, it's Alison. Do you think you could watch the girls for a couple of hours? I have to make an emergency trip downtown."

"Hmm... sure. Are you leaving right away?"

"I want to catch the 3:35, and if I hurry, I think I can make it."

"Okey-doke, Alison. I'll be right over."

Belinda turned up five minutes later, and I zoomed out the door, headed for the commuter train station. I could get there in less than ten minutes if I ran all the way.

I arrived at the station, totally out of breath, just as the 3:35 pulled in, and I hopped on for my 31-minute ride to downtown Chicago.

* * *

Judy met me at The Coffee Spot two minutes after I called from a pay phone downstairs. I felt a bit out-of-place back in the city. Although I'd worked in downtown Chicago in the past, my life in East Winnette was now almost totally removed from life downtown.

"What's happening, Ali? You look kind of frantic."

Judy sat down across from me, looking anything but frantic. She was wearing a chic black suit with a lavender silk blouse and a large silver pin on her jacket lapel. It looked vaguely like a swan. Her shiny brown hair, neatly styled, gleamed under the ceiling lights.

"There's a lot to tell you, Judy."

"So tell me." Judy's bright green eyes (which I'd always envied) were riveted on my less exciting hazel ones.

I sketched in most of the details as quickly as I could. Judy seemed to grasp everything I said. She gasped once or twice at the more shocking details I disclosed. Finally, I began to ask the hard questions.

"Judy, I can't help thinking that Frank Durkin is the most obvious suspect. What do you think?"

"Well, he appears to have had a real motive to kill Kay. If this woman, his receptionist...."

"Thelma Eisenmayer."

"Yes," Judy said. "If she overheard them correctly, Kay wasn't just a garden-variety ex-lover. She was a woman scorned. She'd become a real threat to Frank's professional reputation, a threat to his livelihood."

"Maybe a threat to his marriage, too. And if Frank loves anything, it's his comfortable existence. He isn't about to let anyone threaten that."

"He claims he was on hospital rounds that morning, right? But you don't think that's an ironclad alibi?" Judy asked.

"Not really. After showing up at the hospital, he could have left at a little past eight o'clock and waited for Kay at the nursery school. It's only ten minutes away. Then, if she still refused to bow quietly out of his life, he could have pulled out a knife and stabbed her. He had the medical expertise to know how to inflict a fatal wound. Not everyone would know that."

"That sounds logical."

"But it's that expertise that bothers me. If he stabbed Kay, why was the wound so messy? He was trained to use medical instruments. Wouldn't he use a knife with more skill than that?"

"You'd think so."

"Something else bothers me even more," I said. "Frank's well known around East Winnette. A lot of his patients are kids at the nursery school. Would he really have risked seeing one of their mothers at the school that morning?"

"Umm...I doubt it," Judy answered.

"Then there's Rella Cox and Betty Thurgood."

"The teachers?"

"Yes."

"I guess both of them had reasons to hate Kay Boyer. But I find it hard to believe that either one hated her enough to kill her," Judy said.

"Well, I'm not so sure. At least about Rella Cox. I *am* willing to scratch Betty Thurgood off my list. She was angry with Kay all right, but that anger arose out of her fondness for Kay. When she talked about what happened twelve years ago, she seemed terribly sad. Either she's truly sorry that she and Kay came to a parting of the ways, or she's a very convincing actress."

"But on balance," Judy said, "you don't really think her capable of murder, do you?"

"No. But Rella Cox...she could be."

"The assistant director?"

"Acting director now. And she certainly stored up a lot of bitterness toward Kay."

"Well, she felt threatened, didn't she? All those years she invested in the nursery school were on the line."

"Right," I agreed. "And she thought it was Kay's greed that put her job at risk. Kay had succumbed to the all-American love of money. At least that's how Rella saw it."

"Still," I added, "we're talking about murder, and I have trouble seeing Rella as a murderer. I doubt she'd go that far."

"Then forget her for a minute. Who else is there?"

"There's Jack Hines."

"The guy they arrested?"

"Yes."

"Well? Can you really dismiss him as a suspect?"

"No, I can't. He's done a pretty good job of protesting his innocence, but I can't forget he has a history of criminal behavior."

"It's not just history, Ali. Isn't he still involved in drug-dealing? And didn't he steal some money from the school?"

I nodded. "Kay might have discovered he was stealing that money–and was back to dealing drugs, too. Maybe she arranged to meet him early that morning at the nursery school and told him he was fired.

"She might have added that she was thinking of going to the police. If he felt threatened, maybe he pulled out his knife and killed her."

"It's plausible, Ali. Isn't that the theory the police are going on?"

"Yes." I thought briefly about Joanne Persky. Jack had treated her pretty shabbily, but that didn't seem relevant right now.

"Is there anybody else?"

"There's Gabriel Kidd."

"The Kidd's Korner guy?"

"Right. I'm not sure what to think about him, Judy. When the moment came to sign a contract with Kay, he didn't have the bucks. So he couldn't offer Kay anything but stock in his company. And that stock isn't worth much anymore."

I suddenly remembered that I was meeting with Neal Bannister in a few hours to learn even more about Kidd's Korner. I had to hold off my final judgment on Gabriel Kidd until I heard what Neal had to say. But Judy jumped to the same conclusion I'd reached earlier.

"Here's a possible scenario, Ali. Maybe they scheduled a meeting to finalize their arrangement at eight o'clock Tuesday morning," she said. "Kidd could have stopped off in Chicago en route to his appearance at noon in Detroit–Detroit's less than an hour away by plane. Kay needed, and expected, a cash deal from him. When he told her he didn't have it, she might have gone nuts, even hurling personal insults at him."

"And...?"

"Maybe he reacted badly. Don't most men carry around something like a Swiss army knife? A guy like him might own one of the big ones. He could have pulled it out and stabbed her with it. Manslaughter, of course, not premeditated murder, under those circumstances."

"That's possible."

"And that could account for the messy wound."

"It could..."

"So who's left, Ali?"

"Kay's daughter, Bree–I told you her story. Kay's son, Wes, the one who owns the record store. And her husband, Tom."

"What a bunch," Judy said. "I don't know. Could either of her kids have killed her? You've met them, I haven't."

"Wes? I don't think so. When I saw him, he talked about his mother in positive terms. But it was pretty hard to tell how he really felt. Maybe underneath he's still seething with pain over the way she put the nursery school first, leaving her own kids to shift for themselves while she devoted herself to the kids at her school."

"And Bree?"

"God, I hate to even think about Bree. That poor tormented girl was capable of anything, up to and including murder. But if she was going to kill anyone, wouldn't she have killed her father? He was the monster in her life. Why would she murder her mother when her father was a much more compelling target?"

"Wait a minute, Ali. I know something about incest, remember?"

"You do?" Was Judy about to reveal some terrible secret of her own?

"Don't you remember? I wrote my third-year paper about it. For my criminal law seminar."

I had absolutely no recollection of Judy's third-year paper. All Harvard law students got obsessive over their third-year papers, a requirement for graduation, but the only one I remembered anything about was my own.

"I don't remember it," I admitted. "Sorry."

"I learned a lot about incest when I did research for that paper, and I've read some of the studies that have come out since then. There's much more awareness of it now, of how common it is, and how it happens a lot more in middle-class homes than we thought."

Judy appeared to know what she was talking about. My knowledge of the area was minimal, confined to what I'd learned from the mass media.

"One thing you've got to remember is that the victim frequently blames herself," she said. "The man—say, her father—sometimes convinces her that she seduced him, that she likes it, and that she wants it to go on."

"Bree said something like that."

"I'm not surprised. And even if the girl thinks of her father as a monster, she sometimes blames her mother, too. She thinks her mother should have been aware of what was happening, that she should have seen what the father was doing and should have stopped it."

"Bree said something like that, too."

"Incest victims have a lot of ambivalent feelings, Ali. Bree should get some counseling right away. Especially now with her mother gone. Imagine all the turmoil she's going through."

"I'll see if I can persuade her to get counseling. But...."

"But?"

"But I still need to find Kay's murderer. Do you think, knowing what we know right now, that Bree could have killed her mother?"

Judy paused before speaking again. "Bree must have felt tremendously ambivalent about her mother. Even if deep down she really loved her. When Bree told her mother about Tom, maybe Kay's initial reaction really was disbelief. Maybe she was so revolted that she refused to believe it. Some mothers react that way."

"So do you think Kay accused Bree of lying?"

"She might have. She might have even blamed Bree for initiating what happened. Some mothers do that, too," Judy said. "They accuse their daughters of seducing their husbands."

"God, that's awful. That would have made Bree feel horrible."

"Right. And apparently Bree thought her mother was responsible, at least in part, for what happened. That her mother knew—or should have known—what was happening, and should have helped her."

"So...?"

"So Bree may have boiled over, Ali. Telling her mother what happened, after burying it for so long—she may have been overwhelmed by her feelings. She may have struck out at her mother in a sort of blind rage."

I suddenly remembered something else. I pictured a small six-year-old girl opening a door. A little girl Missy's age.

"Judy, there's something else. Bree was worried about her niece Emily. If Kay's reaction was to deny everything, including what happened to Emily, could that have pushed Bree over the edge?"

"Maybe." Judy paused again. "But there's a missing link here, Ali."

"A missing link?"

"Tom Boyer. You haven't really talked to him. His part in all of this is critical. You need to talk to him."

Judy was right. I had to talk to Tom, to hear from him what had happened that Monday night. If I could get him to talk to me.

First I had to find him....

Suddenly I remembered the time. I looked at my watch. The next train to East Winnette was leaving in six minutes.

I gave Judy a big hug. She'd been a great sounding board. I ran to catch the train for East Winnette and made it with only seconds to spare.

CHAPTER 26

Back home, I thanked Belinda Copeland for her help, then tried calling the Boyers' number again. The phone rang twenty, thirty rings each time I called, and no one ever picked up.

The rain clouds I'd noticed earlier had ripened into heavy dark masses that began to release torrents of rain about dinnertime. After Marv got home and we all shared a quick dinner (spaghetti again), I sat down to watch a Halloween cartoon special with the girls. They giggled through the whole thing, relishing the antics of the Peanuts characters in the old chestnut about the Great Pumpkin. I'd seen it countless times, but it still made me laugh.

Another Halloween special went on, and I wandered into the breakfast room, where Marv was writing up class notes.

"How's it going?" I asked.

"Okay. Just finishing up some notes for the rest of the week."

"Great," I said, trying to think of an artful way to leave the house. "Oh, I just remembered! Don't we need some shampoo—the kind the girls use?"

"I don't know, Alison." Marv looked puzzled. Why was I asking him about Johnson's Baby Shampoo? He was a faithful devotee of Head & Shoulders. "You usually keep track of that stuff, don't you?"

"Yeah, I guess I do," I agreed. Now that I'd set it up, it was time for my ploy. "I think Walgreen's has it on sale. Maybe I'll go out and get it now, while it's still on sale."

"Tonight? In this rain?"

"Well, the sale ends tonight. And I want to stock up."

"If you really want to, go ahead. Just be careful driving." I was right to count on Marv's total lack of interest in shopping. He'd forgotten, as I figured he would, that sales at Walgreen's didn't end till Wednesday.

"I'll get going now," I said. "Do you need anything?"

"Umm, let's see.... Maybe some aftershave. I'm running low."

"Okay," I said, slipping into my slicker. "I'll look for some while I'm there. I, uh, might look for some other stuff, too, so don't worry if I'm gone for a while."

"Okay, sweetness. Just be careful driving," Marv repeated as I closed the back door and walked through several burgeoning puddles toward the Toyota.

I was feeling slightly guilty about lying to Marv as I backed the Toyota out of the gravel-covered space and headed for Walgreen's. But I wasn't doing anything I had to hide from Marv. I just didn't want to bother him with every new development in the murder case.

I knew I'd have to hurry to get in and out of Walgreen's before eight o'clock, then dash over to Neal's office next door, and still get home before Marv would start worrying and the girls would start looking for me to tuck them in bed. I drove as fast as the slick pavement allowed, zipped through Walgreen's at a record pace, and got to Neal's office building a couple of minutes after eight.

The entrance was unlocked. Neal had taped a message to the office directory just inside the door. "Alison: Meet me in

Suite 140." Underneath he'd drawn an arrow pointing left, so I turned left and followed the dimly-lit hallway until I found Suite 140. A plaque on the door said "Bannister Investments, Inc." I knocked.

"Alison, come in, the door's unlocked." Neal's voice was upbeat, confident. That had to mean he'd come across some useful information about Kidd's Korner. My palms were a bit sweaty as I turned the doorknob, excited at the prospect of the new info.

Neal was perched on a metal desk in the center of the room, leafing through some papers. He put down the papers and came towards me, reaching for my slicker. "What a night! I was afraid you might change your mind about coming."

His hands brushed against my arms as he removed my slicker and hung it on a coat tree in a corner of the office. Was I imagining it, or did I tremble—just a little—when he touched me?

Neal rejoined me and led me to a plump upholstered sofa along the far wall of the office. I sank into its depths while he retrieved the papers he'd left on his desk. "Is that the information you found?" I asked.

"Yep, this is it," Neal said. He sank down into the sofa next to me. His clear blue eyes looked into mine. "It's not much, Alison, but it's something."

I looked at the stack of papers he handed me. It was a photocopy of an article from *Business Week*. A month-old article about the day-care industry. I leafed through it eagerly, looking for Gabriel Kidd's name. It finally appeared in a short paragraph that said even less about Kidd's Korner than the articles in the *Wall Street Journal* I'd read in the library.

"Is this it, Neal?" I asked, feeling distinctly let down. I'd expected much more.

"That's it," he admitted. "I'm sorry, but I couldn't find anything else." He must have noticed the let-down look on my face. "I tried to find more," he added. "I just couldn't."

The sheepish look on Neal's face was endearing. It was hard to get terribly angry with him. "But Neal, you could have put this in the mail. I thought you'd have something... something I had to see right away."

"I do, Alison." His voice was suddenly softer, huskier.

"You do?" I was confused. "Where is it?"

"It's right here," he said, putting his arm around my waist. "It's me."

I was too startled to move. "Neal...I don't...I...."

Neal pulled me toward him and encircled me with his other arm. "I want you, Alison. I need you," he breathed into my ear. Then he pressed his lips against mine.

I struggled to push him away, to rise from the depths of the sofa, but I failed. Neal was holding me so tightly I couldn't move.

I turned my face away as he tried to kiss me again. I didn't know what to do, what to say. "What about Mary Beth, Neal?" I said finally. I thought of Mary Beth's heart-shaped face, her frizzy brown hair. Did Neal have a thing for women with frizzy hair?

"Mary Beth?" Neal loosened his grasp on me at the sound of his wife's name. I seized the opportunity to pull myself out of the sofa, stand up, and move towards the door. Neal rose immediately and followed me. His arms reached out and enveloped me again.

"Mary Beth's a great girl, Alison, but...but after ten years of marriage, well, the spark's gone. You must know what I mean." Neil began nuzzling my neck. Suddenly my knees felt weak. My reflexes took over, and I put my arms around him to steady myself.

Neal interpreted this as encouragement. Maybe it was. He kissed me again, and I felt myself responding. He was right, of course. After ten or twelve years of marriage, the pulse-pounding, heart-throbbing novelty of a new romance has faded.

Sure, Marv and I still shared plenty of spark. Our encounter in the bedroom Saturday night had proved that. But Marv's kisses were sweet, gentle, familiar. Neal's kisses were different—demanding, intense. And my response to them shocked me. Suddenly I was kissing him back with the same intensity, the same excitement.

Almost without my noticing it, Neal began directing me back towards the sofa. He pushed me down onto it gently, and lay himself on top of me. His hands reached under my sweater and groped behind me to unhook my bra. I was breathless. I tried to catch my breath while he moved his lips to my neck again.

One of his hands came around to touch my breasts under my sweater. "Alison, you're beautiful. I want you," he whispered into my ear, one hand caressing my breasts, the other grasping me close to him. His lips pressed against mine again.

I closed my eyes. Should I, could I, let this happen? Surrendering to Neal's desires, to his needs...I knew it wasn't right. But I had to admit that my body was responding to him, probably a lot more than it should have.

Our lips separated, and Neal began to kiss my neck again. I turned my face, my eyes searching for his. But before our eyes met, mine fell on a clock hanging on the wall. 8:25. The number registered in my brain, and a few seconds later, it brought me back to reality. 8:25.

Now the clock said 8:26. Almost 8:30.

I'd left the house nearly an hour ago. Marv would be looking out the window, watching for my car. The girls would be asking where I was. I had to get home, I had to stop, I had to....

"Neal," I breathed. "Neal, I can't." I struggled to free myself from his embrace.

He looked at me, shock and frustration spreading across his face. "What? Alison...."

"I know, Neal, I know," I said, pulling away from him, standing up, shaky, confused. "I shouldn't have let things get this far. I'm sorry, I really am. I just...I just can't do this."

Neal was sitting up on the sofa, shaking his head. "I thought you felt something for me—the way you looked at me, the way you responded to me...."

"I guess I did...I did respond to you, Neal. I'm...I'm surprised myself at what happened. But I just...I just can't... I have to get home, the girls are waiting, and Marv, and I...I..."

I was babbling. The abrupt end to our frenzied groping had left me incoherent. "Maybe...maybe some other...."

I couldn't complete that thought. Removed now from his arms, I didn't think I would ever let myself fall into them again.

I turned and ran out of the office. Outside the building entrance, viewing the torrents of rain, I realized I'd left my slicker in Neal's office. But I couldn't go back.

I dashed to the car, getting soaked, and drove home. I felt flushed, almost feverish, and a plan came to mind. I'd tell Marv I got hot in Walgreen's, took off my slicker, and forgot it there.

It suddenly hit me. Tell Marv that, during my hour away from him, I got hot? I immediately became convulsed with hysterical laughter.

Clearly, I was shaken by what had happened. I was feeling frantic, reflecting on how close I'd come to jeopardizing the life I had with Marv.

Alone in the Toyota, shivering, I laughed frenetically all the way home.

CHAPTER 27

I found an old parka in the trunk of the car and threw it on, covering up my wet clothes. Marv looked happy to see me when I walked through the back door. "I was worried about you, sweetness," he said. "What took so long?"

I told him a hastily contrived version of my shopping trip. "I had to get a raincheck for the shampoo," I lied. "The clerk took forever."

In exchange for my deceitful story, I got a lovely kiss. "I'm just glad you're okay," Marv said.

I realized once again how lucky I was to have a wonderful guy like Marv. He'd been concerned about me while I was grappling on a sofa with another man.

I quickly ran downstairs to the laundry room, stripped off my wet clothes, and pulled some clean clothes out of the dryer for something to wear. Upstairs again, I helped Marv get the girls ready for bed.

Marv headed for bed a short time later, and I cleaned up the kitchen before heading upstairs myself. When I finally climbed under the covers, he was already snoring gently. But I couldn't fall asleep.

A raft of images swirled through my head. I tried to put Neal out of my mind, but it wasn't easy. I closed my eyes, but I kept seeing Neal's face, feeling his lips warm against mine, his arms tightening around me....

Marv turned over in his sleep, and I glanced at him. Marv. Wonderful Marv. How could I jeopardize a dozen years' worth of love, genuine love, that we'd shared? It was suddenly unthinkable.

Who needed Butch Cassidy? I already had the Sundance Kid. Those few minutes in Neal's arms were a crazy offshoot of this whole crazy detective business. When Neal called to tell me he had new information about Kidd's Korner, I promptly fell into his carefully prepared trap. I wondered how many other women in East Winnette had fallen into one of Neal's traps.

He'd made it so easy, so easy to fall. I was shocked at how I'd nearly succumbed. Thank God I'd had the sense to pull myself out of his arms before it went any further.

When I finally managed to shunt thoughts of Neal aside, Kay's murder leaped in to fill the void. Bree Boyer's story of her incestuous ordeal, Frank Durkin's smug confidences, the other revelations of the past week.... What did it all mean?

I tried to remember everything Judy had said, hoping to tie it together with Kay's murder. But there was still too much I didn't understand.

Towards morning I slept an hour or two, awakening about six o'clock. I dressed quietly and went downstairs.

I made myself a pot of coffee and looked outside. Another misty morning. Just like Tuesday morning a week ago. The words of the children's song came into my head: "One misty, moisty morning, when cloudy was the weather, I chanced to meet an old man...."

"An old man...."

I suddenly had an idea. Maybe it didn't make much sense, but I had to check it out. I found my jacket, grabbed my car keys, and left the house. The usual mist covered the Toyota's windshield. I cleared it with the wipers and drove off.

The nursery school was deserted when I got there. The door wasn't locked, and I walked right in. I couldn't help shaking as I walked through the dark hallway toward the classroom where Kay Boyer was murdered.

When I got to the threshold of the classroom, I peered inside. My heart was racing, and my hands had turned ice cold. I thought I saw a shadowy figure sitting in the farthest corner of the room.

I entered the room as quietly as I could and slowly walked toward the figure.

"Tom?" I said softly.

"Who's there?" Tom Boyer said. "Who is it?"

"It's Alison Ross," I said, trying to keep my voice steady. "I came to talk to you."

"Oh, it's you." He seemed to recognize me in the dim light. "I remember you. Your name is Alison. I talked to you at the house, didn't I?"

"That's right, Tom. And now, can we talk again? Can we talk about Kay?"

"About Kay?" he repeated. I pulled over a kid-sized chair and seated myself close to him. "Why?" he asked.

"That's why you're here, isn't it, Tom? Because of Kay?"

"But why do you want to talk about Kay?"

I had to think of some kind of response. A response that wouldn't scare him off. Even in the dim light, he seemed so fragile, so unstable. Ready to stop talking at any moment.

"Because I cared about Kay, Tom. And I care about you."

"You care about me?" he said with a look of disbelief. "Nobody cares about me. My kids...my kids used to...but... but they don't anymore."

Sure, I thought. You thought your daughters loved you, didn't you, Tom? Until one of them hanged herself and the other one finally pushed you away.

"But I care, Tom," I repeated. If I kept saying that, maybe he'd disclose something helpful. "I want to make sure you're okay. I really do."

In a sense, I really did want that. I wanted him to be okay, to be stable enough to be held accountable for what he'd done to his daughters. For what he'd threatened to do to Emily.

After a minute or two, Tom began to speak again. "This was Kay's school, you know," he said. "This was the place Kay liked best."

"Was it?"

"Kay liked this place better than our own house. She liked the kids here better than our own kids," he said sadly.

"Why do you say that, Tom?"

"Because she always wanted to be here. Not at home with our kids. Not at home with me." His voice drifted off.

"It's hard to be a good parent," I said. "I know. I'm a parent, too. You and I have that in common, Tom. We love our kids, don't we? But sometimes it's hard to know what to do. Hard to do right thing."

"Yes, that's right, Alison." He half-smiled at me, acknowledging that we, as parents, shared a similar burden.

"I'm sure Kay wanted to be home with you and your kids, Tom. She just got so wrapped up in this school...."

"You don't understand," Tom interrupted. His voice was suddenly stronger, angrier. "She chose this school over us. And you know what happened...."

"What happened, Tom?" I asked gently. I didn't want him to be angry with me, so angry he'd stop talking.

"Once she started this school, she never wanted to be with me. Even when she came home, she ignored me. I wondered sometimes if she cared about me at all. She'd dream up one excuse after another to avoid being with me. It was always the school, the school...."

"So you turned to the children, didn't you, Tom? First to Julie, then to Bree...."

"Yes, of course I did! Where else could I turn? I needed someone to love me, someone I could love...."

"Why didn't you turn to Wes, Tom?" I asked. I had to be sure.

"Wes? Hah! He was always off playing some game or other. A real jock!" He almost laughed at the thought of his son, the athlete. "No, not Wes. I always wanted to be with the girls...."

Yes, I thought, that much is clear. "What happened last Monday night, Tom?" I asked. "Do you remember? What happened when Kay talked to you last Monday?" I was bluffing, but I had no choice. I had to know if my suspicions were right.

"Last Monday?" he echoed. "The night before Kay died?"

"Yes."

"You mean the night...the night Kay accused me of...of sleeping with our daughters?"

"Yes, Tom." So Kay had confronted him, just as she'd told Bree she would.

"I told her they wanted it as much as I did. They did, you know. They did." He was trying to convince himself as much as me. "They wanted it. They loved me, and they wanted to go to bed with me. They wanted the love only a father can give a young girl."

His rationalization for the way he'd preyed upon his daughters revolted me. In my eyes, it was nothing short of rape. "And now Emily...Emily wants it, too. She's just like the others," he insisted. "I love her, and she loves me. She wants to go to bed with me, too."

I felt ill. How could I continue talking to this monster? This warped father who had manipulated and destroyed the well-being of his own daughters?

I forced myself to keep talking. "What did Kay say?"

He paused. "She said she couldn't believe it, she couldn't believe Bree was telling the truth. That it had gone on for so long and she'd never suspected...."

"What did you say?"

"I said Bree had told her the truth."

"Did Kay seem shocked to hear it?"

He nodded.

"But you told her that Julie and Bree both loved you, that they wanted to do it?"

"Yes, of course I did!"

"Did she...did she blame Bree for seducing you?"

Tom's eyes shifted away from me. He didn't answer.

"What did Kay say?" I repeated.

He looked back at me. A strange look crept over his deeply-lined face. "Yes, she blamed Bree. No...no..., wait a minute." He shook his head and paused before speaking again. "She blamed me. Me. She said I was a pervert, a criminal."

"You must have been angry when she called you those names. What did you do?"

"I told her she was wrong. My daughters wanted to be close to me. They loved me. Even Julie...." Grief replaced the anger on his face. "My Julie...." He slowly rose from his chair and walked over to the window. The sun was coming up, and light had begun to stream into the room.

I had to get him back on track. "You were angry with Kay, weren't you, Tom? She called you those names. You were angry with her when she said those things to you."

Tom nodded.

"And you were still angry with her the next morning, weren't you?"

Tom turned back to look at me. In the morning light, his face had a weird, almost deranged look. He slowly walked back toward me and collapsed into his chair. "We were up all night, Alison. Talking. Going back and forth over everything that happened. I finally left. Went out for a walk," he said. "I walked for hours, down the dark streets near our house. When I got back, she was gone.

"I knew where she had gone. Here. Where else did she ever want to go?"

"And then, Tom?"

"I wanted to go after her. To explain everything again. Maybe she'd believe me if I explained everything again."

"Did you go after her, Tom?"

He hesitated. Then his back straightened, and his chin jutted out towards me. He began to talk again. "Yes. I followed her here in my car. I...." He stopped again.

"Go on, Tom," I prodded.

"I thought if I could talk to her again, tell her how it really was between the girls and me, how much we loved each other, maybe she'd understand."

"Is that what happened, Tom? Were you able to make her understand?"

He shook his head. "When I got here, she wouldn't talk to me. She told me to save it for the police. She told me to my face, 'Save it for the police.' I couldn't let that happen...."

"No, of course you couldn't, Tom. You couldn't let her go to the police."

"You understand, don't you?" He looked at me. The light coming through the window was brighter now, and I could see his face more clearly. It was a face marked by weariness, mixed with a weird sort of grief. "You understand, don't you?" he repeated.

"Tell me what happened then, Tom."

"I had to do something...I had to do something. She called me a pervert...."

He stopped talking. Maybe he couldn't face the truth. I had to help him say it.

"You killed her, didn't you, Tom? You had to kill her, or she would have told the police."

Tom Boyer's grief-filled face turned away from me. He looked toward the window and began to speak again without looking at me. "That's right, Alison. That's right. You under-stand, don't you? I had to kill her. I had to kill Kay...."

"How did you do it, Tom?"

He was silent. "How did you do it?" I repeated.

"I...I grabbed a knife," he said.

"Where did you get a knife?"

He looked around the room. "I took one from over there," he said. "It was in a drawer next to the sink, over there." He pointed to the small sink in the opposite corner of the room. "Kay used that knife to cut up the children's food. Oranges and apples, homemade bread."

I nodded. "What did you do with the knife, Tom?"

"I...I took it and I stuck it in her," he said. "I stuck it in her. And then she fell into the chest. The one with all those old clothes. She fell into the chest."

"What happened then?"

"She fell into the chest...." His voice drifted off.

"But after that, after she fell into the chest, what did you do?" I asked. He said nothing. "You left her in the chest and you went home, didn't you?"

"Yes, yes," he said after a moment. "I went home."

"And the knife, Tom? What did you do with the knife?" I asked.

He hesitated for a moment. Then he spoke again. "I washed it off, here, at the sink. Then I took it home with me. It's in a drawer in the kitchen. It's right there in a drawer." He paused. "I had to do it, you know. I had to. You understand, don't you, Alison? You understand...."

"Yes, yes, I do. I understand," I said. "Just rest now, Tom. I'll be right back."

Tom had summoned up all his energy to tell me his story. Now he seemed to collapse, his body slumping over in the chair, his strength sapped.

I knew he could try to get away, but I didn't think he would.

I left the room and looked for the nearest phone. I remembered the one in the supply room, next to the cabinet.

It was there, just where I remembered it. I picked it up and called the police.

CHAPTER 28

The police arrived at the nursery school almost immediately. Bob Shakespear wasn't among them, but I told the officers who showed up to notify Bob.

The officers treated Tom carefully as they guided him to their car. He seemed drained and barely able to function, and I wondered what the police would do with him once they booked him at the station.

I headed for home and got back by eight o'clock. Marv and the girls were having breakfast.

"Where were you, Mommy?" Missy asked.

"Tell you later, sweetheart," I answered, pouring myself a cup of coffee.

Marv looked up at me. I could tell he suspected that something significant had just happened. He also seemed to sense that I didn't want to talk about it in front of the girls. While I got Missy off to school, he reminded me that he had no classes on Wednesdays, and he offered to watch Lindsay all morning so I could rest. I gave him a grateful kiss, then headed upstairs to bed.

But although I lay in bed for a while, I never fell asleep. My mind was busy, thinking about Tom Boyer and his confession. That pathetic, hateful old man. Driven by guilt and fear of exposure into killing the wife he loved, or claimed to love. Now he was not only exposed as the abuser of his daughters, something he'd hidden for so long, but he'd also become something far worse—a murderer.

Or was it really worse? I wasn't sure. A man who forces sex on his daughters, who drives one of them to suicide and the other to an existence forever traumatized by what he did— maybe he amounted to a murderer in another sense.

Something about Tom's confession was bothering me, but I couldn't figure out what it was. Everything seemed to fall into place all right. Tom certainly had a motive, and he'd clearly explained how he'd found and used the murder weapon. But there was something about what he'd said that troubled me, and I didn't know why.

I went downstairs to find Marv, to see if he could help me think things through. But the house was deserted. I found a note attached to the refrigerator door with a magnet:

Alison:
    We've gone to the library. See you later.
    M.

I had to talk to somebody. I tried calling Judy, but she was in court, so I called Bob Shakespear instead. It took him several minutes to come to the phone.

"Alison?"

"Bob, what's happening?"

"We're pretty busy here. Taking down Tom Boyer's statement and doing all the rest of the paperwork." He sounded frazzled.

"Can I do anything to help?"

"No, no, it's just routine police work," he said. "By the way, how did you get him to confess? We couldn't get very much out of the old guy. He seemed so torn up about his wife's death, and it seemed so genuine."

"Did you talk to his daughter Bree? Or his son Wes?"

"Sure," he said. "But they didn't have much to say either. The whole family just seemed so shocked, and so upset, we couldn't see them as suspects."

I paused. I didn't want to offend Bob. How could I explain to him—without gloating–that I was able to come up with the real killer when the police weren't?

"That family is a mess," I said finally. "But it wasn't easy to figure out what happened. I had to spend a lot of time with them. I had to ask a lot of questions."

"Looks that way," he said. "Listen, I gotta run. But before I forget, your buddy's been released."

"My buddy?"

"Jack Hines," Bob said. "We let him go about twenty minutes ago."

"Oh." Jack Hines. I'd totally forgotten about him.

"He really owes you a lot," Bob said. "I wonder if he realizes how much."

"Well, I was responsible for your arresting him in the first place. So I really owed it to *him*."

"Maybe so," Bob said. "But not many people would do what you did for him. Especially a stranger. Especially one like him."

"He's not that bad a guy, is he?" I asked. "After a while, I kind of liked the idea of helping him. Once I found out what was really going on in Kay Boyer's life, I felt sorry for him."

"You felt sorry for him?" Bob sounded dubious that anyone could feel sorry for Jack Hines.

"Sure. He was a classic case of someone who's falsely accused of a crime because of circumstantial evidence. It was practically out of a B movie."

"Maybe." Bob didn't sound convinced, but as we talked, I was beginning to feel almost sympathetic toward Jack Hines. I thought I might even want to get in touch with him sometime.

"Bob, do you know how I can reach him?"

"Who? Jack Hines?"

"Yeah," I said.

"You want his phone number?"

"Yeah." Maybe I'd give Jack a call and bask for a while in his gratitude.

"Wait a second," Bob said. "I'll get his file." A moment later he came back on the phone. "We don't have a phone number for him. Just an address. He probably doesn't have a phone."

"Oh. Well, can you give me his address?" I could always drop him a note and ask him to call me.

Bob gave me an address on the far north side of Chicago, a furnished apartment-hotel near Loyola University. I was famil-iar with that neighborhood. My elderly great-aunt had lived there, and I remembered visiting her apartment several times before she died.

"Thanks, Bob," I said. "I may get in touch with him sometime."

"I wouldn't do that if I were you," Bob said.

"Why not?"

"He's not a very nice boy, you know. Leave him alone."

Maybe Bob was right. We said goodbye, promising to keep in touch.

I poured myself a Diet Pepsi and glanced through the morning newspaper. But it was impossible to concentrate on news from the Middle East and Southeast Asia. I had too much on my mind right here in East Winnette.

Why wasn't I comfortable with the way the case had turned out? Why couldn't I stop thinking about Kay Boyer's murder and her husband's admitted role as her killer?

I decided to get my mind off the murder and go shopping. I wanted to check out Halloween costumes for the girls, and today was as good as any to look for them. I grabbed my purse to make sure my credit card was there.

I found what I needed, plus something else: Frank Durkin's well-worn address book, still hidden away in my purse, forgotten ever since I'd stashed it there.

Oh my God, I thought. I have to return this book to Frank's desk. But how?

I couldn't help flipping through the book again, returning to the page with "KB" written on it. I was sure now that was the nursery school's phone number.

I glanced at some of the other entries on the page, and suddenly my heart stopped. Just below "KB," Frank had scribbled "JH" with an address that leaped off the page at me. It was the address for Jack Hines I'd just gotten from Bob Shakespear.

I tried to calm down and think. Why would Frank Durkin have Jack Hines's address listed in his book? And why would it be on the "B" page, just below Kay Boyer's phone number, instead of on the "H" page, where it belonged?

None of this made any sense. How did Frank Durkin come to know Jack Hines? Had they met at the nursery school? Had Jack found out about Frank's liaison with Kay and tried his hand at blackmail? Or was there some innocent explanation?

Maybe Frank simply needed some maintenance work at his house, and Kay recommended her school's janitor as a reliable worker. Frank could have jotted down Jack's address under

Kay's as a reminder that she recommended him. The connection between Frank and Jack could be as simple as that.

I put the address book back in my purse. Now that Tom Boyer had confessed, the book didn't really matter anymore. Kay's affair with Frank turned out to have no connection to her murder. So the best thing to do right now would be to return the address book.

I could go shopping, as planned. On my way to the store, I could drive by Frank's house and put the address book back.

But just how could I do that? Even if no one was home, and even if the sliding glass doors were open (and I wasn't sure they would be), I'd risk being discovered again. I couldn't use that story about the pool-cleaning service a second time. Barbara Durkin would know I was lying.

Maybe…maybe it wasn't a good idea to return the address book to Frank's desk after all. Maybe it would still help the police to know that Kay had been involved with Frank Durkin.

Besides, that notation of Jack Hines's initials and address was something else to consider. What exactly was the connection between them?

It was ridiculous, of course, but I couldn't focus on anything else till I knew the answer to that question. I went to the phone and tried calling Frank Durkin's office. I got his answering service, so I left a message asking Frank to call me.

Next I tried calling B. Durkin at 225 Forest Drive. I let the phone ring for a long time, but no one answered. Damn! Now I'd never know.

Then I realized there was something else I could do. It was the only thing left to do. I could try to talk to Jack Hines.

* * *

I left the house and pointed the Toyota south towards the city. I took Sheridan Road all the way, through East Winnette and Evanston, passing the Baha'i temple, the Northwestern campus, and the huge old homes along the way. The lake, when I caught a glimpse of it, was turquoise blue in the sunlight. The misty morning had turned into a beautiful fall day.

Sheridan Road entered Chicago just past a big cemetery near the lake. I stayed on Sheridan, impatiently weaving through the congested traffic that appeared as soon as I crossed the city limits. Drab apartment buildings and nursing homes, mom-and-pop stores and pizza parlors filled the twenty blocks or so before I reached Devon Avenue and the turn where Sheridan Road began to morph into a posh neighborhood of high-rise condominiums.

I turned, then turned again onto a side street a block before that metamorphosis. Some furnished apartment-hotels fronted the street, along with other apartment buildings and a scattering of old houses. The neighborhood was looking better than I'd remembered. Maybe this was another rundown section of the city that was beginning to gentrify.

I found Jack Hines's building right away. It was one of the seedier buildings, and I doubted whether even massive renovation efforts could turn it around. I searched for a parking space nearby and circled the block until I finally found one. After checking that the Toyota's doors were securely locked, I walked back to Jack's building.

The hotel lobby was dimly lit and smelled as though fresh air was a rare and unattainable commodity. An old man in a washed-out plaid shirt sat in a dilapidated upholstered chair, reading yesterday's *Sun-Times*. He looked like one of the pathetic old guys who extracted their reading matter from city trash cans before the trash collectors could get their hands on it. When recycling really takes off, I thought, these guys will have nothing to read.

Mr. Plaid looked up at me vacantly, then went back to his newspaper.

I looked around and finally noticed a fancy wooden reception desk in an alcove along one wall. The wood was badly scarred, but it was evidence that the hotel had been an elegant place in its day.

No one was seated at the desk.

"Hello?" I called. "Is anyone working here?" I glanced around. I needed help to find Jack Hines. "Hello?" I called again.

At last I heard a door open. Someone said, "Hold your horses, hold your horses, I'm comin'." An enormously overweight woman of indeterminate age waddled toward me. Her bright orange hair was set in pink plastic rollers, waiting for some unknown event she deemed worthy enough to comb it out.

"What is it?" she asked, not even trying to keep the annoyance out of her voice.

"I'm looking for Jack Hines," I said. "Can you tell me which apartment he lives in?"

The woman made her way into the alcove and consulted a smudged list taped to the wall.

"Jack Hines, Jack Hines," she said. "To be."

"To be?" I asked. "To be what?"

"To be," she repeated. "Apartment to be." Her enormous jowls began to quiver with impatience.

All at once I realized what she meant. "You mean Apartment 2-B, right?"

"Right," she said. She scowled at me and began to waddle out of the alcove. Then she turned and added, "But you can't take the elevator. It's broke. You gotta take those stairs." She pointed a hefty arm toward a staircase. I could barely see it in the dim light, but I walked toward it and began to climb the stairs.

"Turn left at the landing," the woman shouted after me.

The marble stairs were covered with threadbare striped carpeting that hadn't seen better days for a long time. I climbed slowly, watching carefully where I put my feet. A liability suit against this place wouldn't be worth the paper it was written on. When I reached the second floor, I turned left. Apartment 2-B was the first apartment on my right.

I hesitated when I approached the door. *Do you really want to do this, Alison? Do you know what you're getting yourself into?* I suddenly remembered what Bob Shakespear had said: Jack Hines was not a very nice boy.

But wasn't I his heroine? I'd saved him from the electric chair, or so he thought. He should be glad to see me.

I assured myself I had nothing to worry about and knocked on the door. I couldn't help noticing that my hand was shaking as I knocked.

"Who is it?" I heard Jack's voice through the door.

"It's Alison Ross, Jack." My voice was shaking, too. "Can I talk to you?"

I heard Jack's footsteps, then the lock turning. Jack opened the door a crack and looked at me through the narrow opening. "What do you want?" he asked. He was unshaven and didn't look the least bit happy to see me. Didn't he remember I was his heroine?

I tried to smile. "Jack, can I talk to you for a minute? I just want to ask you a couple of things."

"You wanna ask me things?" he repeated. "I got nothing to say. The police let me go. What do we got to talk about?"

He was being distinctly unpleasant. I hadn't expected open arms exactly, but I hadn't expected this degree of rudeness, either.

"Please, Jack, can I come in for a minute? It'll only take a minute, I promise."

He peered at me through narrowed eyes. He seemed to be deciding what to do. Then he silently opened the door some more, and I walked into his apartment.

It was dark and dingy, with clothes and papers lying haphazardly on every conceivable surface. A battered suitcase was propped open on a chipped formica table in the middle of the room. It was halfway filled.

"Are you going away, Jack?" I tried to sound friendly, like someone geniunely interested in him. I didn't want him to think I was questioning him, or threatening him in any way. I didn't know how he'd react if he got angry.

"Yeah, I am," he said. He pushed some stuff off a sofa and sat down. He didn't ask me to join him.

"Well, I don't blame you," I said. "After all that's happened...." I smiled tentatively at him. I was feeling more and more uneasy by the minute. I hoped my friendly demeanor would reassure him.

"Yeah," he said. He paused. "I guess I should thank you for everything." He got out a pack of cigarettes, took one out, and offered the pack to me.

I shook my head. "Well, I just wanted to see justice done. I'm glad everything turned out okay."

"Uh-huh," he grunted. He started to relax, and his mouth suddenly began to curve in a half-smile. It made his otherwise good-looking face look even better. No wonder Joanne Persky had been attracted to him.

"Amazing, how you got that old geezer to confess. Amazing. I really gotta hand it to you." He nodded his head approvingly. "Now what do you wanna ask me?" He lit his cigarette and blew the smoke in my direction.

I walked over to the window and looked outside. The brilliant autumn day was obscured by several years' worth of dirt on the window panes. I decided to get right to the point. "Do you know Dr. Durkin?" I asked, turning to look at Jack again.

"Who?"

"Dr. Durkin. Dr. Frank Durkin," I said, watching his face.

He hesitated. "Why do you want to know?" he asked warily.

"Just curious, Jack," I said. "Someone I know mentioned that you did some work for him." My bluff worked. Jack's face suddenly looked guarded, suspicious.

"What did you say?" he demanded.

"I said I heard you did some work for him—around his house," I said quickly. I tried to think of something that sounded reasonable. "I heard he hired you to clean his pool."

Now Jack's face relaxed again. "Oh, yeah, that's right. I cleaned his pool the other day, right before I was arrested. He liked my work, too."

I knew no one had cleaned the Durkins' pool when Jack said he had. Why had he just told me he did?

"Is that all you wanted to know?" Jack was beginning to look at me suspiciously once more. "You came all the way over here to ask me about Dr. Durkin's pool?" He put out his cigarette in a cheap glass ashtray overflowing with butts.

I tried to laugh. "Of course not, Jack. I just wanted to wish you luck, and tell you how happy I am I could help you get out of jail. You don't have a phone, Jack," I reminded him. "I had to drive over here to talk to you."

Jack got up from the sofa and began putting things in the suitcase. "Well, thanks for your help. Now I'm kinda busy, so if you ain't got nothing else to say...."

I began to walk toward the door. Something was terribly wrong, but I didn't know what. Clearly, the best thing to do was to get out of there. I would sort out everything later.

"Well, goodbye, Jack. I'll say goodbye to Dr. Durkin for you." I opened the door and began to enter the hall. Suddenly I felt Jack Hines grab me by the arm and pull me back into the room. He slammed the door behind me and locked it.

"Okay, bitch! That does it!" he shouted in my face, his cigarette breath blasting me. My heart began pounding so hard, I thought it would leap out of my chest. "You come around here asking questions, asking me about Frank Durkin. Just what do you know, bitch?"

He dragged me over to the sofa and threw me down. I hit my head on the wall behind the sofa, and I suddenly felt dizzy. "I don't know anything, Jack!" I said. "I just came over to say hello." My head was starting to throb with pain. Why had I mentioned Frank Durkin again?

"I bet!" he taunted. "You know something, bitch, and I want to know what it is!" He grabbed my arm again and began twisting it. I screamed, and he slapped me in the face. I felt a burning pain on my cheek like nothing I'd ever felt before.

I began to sob, and I must have gone into some kind of shock because I couldn't stop crying. He slapped my face again, and I thought I would lose consciousness any second.

"Tell me what you know!" he shouted. My head sagged onto my chest. I couldn't believe this was really happening. It had to be a nightmare, like the nightmare Missy had a few weeks before. She woke up screaming, and it took ten minutes of soothing her in my arms before she could fall back to sleep.

Now I wanted to wake up from this nightmare and find myself in bed, being rocked back to sleep in Marv's arms.

Jack grabbed my hair and pulled my head up. "Did Durkin tell you something?" he demanded. "What did that bastard tell you?" He let go of my hair and walked over to the window. "I knew I never should have trusted that bastard. I haven't even seen any of the money he promised. Not one buck," he muttered.

I stopped sobbing and looked over at him. "Frank didn't tell me anything," I said. I felt my cheek puffing up, and the spot where I hit my head was aching. "He didn't tell me anything," I repeated.

"That bastard!" Jack shouted. "That dirty bastard! I'll kill him, too!"

He looked back at me. His face was contorted with rage, and he didn't seem to care what he said to me anymore. "He set me up good, that fucking bastard. He comes over here that night and says he wants me to kill that old bitch. And he gets me to kill her for him. Even though I never killed nobody before."

He sat down on a torn upholstered chair and lighted another cigarette. "Then he sits back when you ID me and the police lock me up. He never even lifted a finger to help me, that motherfucker."

So that was what happened. What really happened. Tom Boyer hadn't killed Kay after all. Jack had. And Jack had killed her because Frank had put him up to it. "Why'd you do it, Jack?" I asked. "I thought Mrs. Boyer was nice to you."

"Oh, yeah, that's what I told everyone." He laughed. "And they believed me! Truth is she was a mean old bitch. She gave me a hard time about that money I took. I didn't owe her nothing."

"So when Frank Durkin asked you to kill her, you were happy to oblige?"

"What? Oh, yeah. Happy to oblige. For ten thousand bucks," he smiled. "Ten thousand bucks I still ain't got." His smile vanished.

"How did you meet Frank Durkin, Jack?" My head was aching, but I could still think clearly. And I wanted to know the answer to this one. "Why did he hire you to kill her?"

"She told him about me," he said. "He wanted help moving his office furniture around. She told him I could do it."

So if Kay hadn't told Frank about Jack Hines, maybe she would still be alive.

"When was that, Jack?"

He thought for a moment. "About a month ago. I went over there one night. He had me move some stuff around. I guess he liked me. He said he might have another job for me sometime."

And he did, I thought. Did he ever. "When did he ask you to kill her, Jack?"

"The night before I did it," he said. "He came over here that night and told me he wanted me to off the bitch. For ten thousand bucks...." Jack's eyes glazed over. He was contemplating the idea of ten thousand dollars. Ten thousand dollars he'd been cheated out of.

"Why didn't you tell the police Frank hired you to kill her?"

"I didn't want to admit nothing to the police. I decided to keep saying I didn't do it. Make the police prove it. They didn't have that much to go on."

"But Frank had hired you...."

"Yeah. But he told me he'd deny it. It'd be his word against mine. Besides, he told me to keep my mouth shut if

I ever wanted to see any of that money. If I ratted on him, I'd get nothing."

He began to pace the room, thinking. He made thinking look hard. Suddenly he looked back at me.

"I got an idea," he said. He was half-smiling again.

My head was throbbing. "Jack, can I have some water, please?" I asked. "And maybe a towel. Something wet I can put on my head. It really hurts."

Jack laughed. "I got a better idea, babe," he said. He paused and waited for my reaction. I didn't move. "I'm gonna take you to the doctor." The half-smile changed to a full one, and he laughed again. "We'll go see the fucking doctor together. He'll fix you up all right."

I tried to stall while I thought of some way to escape before Jack could take me to see Frank Durkin. "What do you mean, Jack? Why would Frank want to see me?"

Jack walked over to a chest and began to open a drawer. What did he have in there? "Oh, I think he'll be real interested to see you," he said. "Real interested."

He rummaged through the drawer but apparently didn't find what he was looking for. He opened another drawer and resumed his search.

I looked around the room, desperate for something to help me get away. The lamp on a side table, the one caked with generations of dust. Did I have the strength to pick it up and swing it at Jack? I didn't think so.

A fat black cockroach crawled across the table and began climbing up the lamp.

Jack was looking in a third drawer now. He pulled out a length of rope, probably intended for me. Then he pushed his hand back into the drawer and felt around for something else.

I glanced over at the pullman kitchen. The stove was encrusted with burnt-on food and other filth I couldn't begin to identify. Above it was a shelf with some canned goods. I thought I saw a bright red spray can that looked familiar.

I got up slowly and walked hesitantly toward the kitchen. "I'm just getting some water, Jack. I've got to have some water," I said, trying to sound weak, non-threatening. It wasn't hard. I felt decidedly weak and non-threatening.

Jack whirled around and looked at me. "What are you doing?" he said. He was watching me carefully now.

"I said I had to get some water, Jack. My head hurts like hell." I walked over to the filthy sink and turned on the faucet. I plunged my hands into the cool water and splashed some on my face.

Jack seemed satisfied and turned away, searching again for whatever it was he wanted. I left the water running and looked at the shelf above the stove. There it was, a large can of Raid bug killer, next to some cans of food. I grabbed it and ran for the door.

I managed to open the lock before Jack noticed I had moved. Then he noticed. He approached me, waving something. I heard a soft clicking sound.

I turned towards him. Then I pointed the can of Raid at him and sprayed it in his face.

He screamed in pain as the spray hit his eyes. He dropped whatever he'd been waving at me and clutched at his eyes with his hands.

The object clattered to the floor. It was a small switchblade knife, its blade shining in the dim light.

I opened the door and fled into the hallway. I headed for the stairway and began to run down the stairs. I could still hear Jack's screams as I ran through the lobby and out onto the street.

I found the Toyota and got inside fast, locking the doors. I was breathing hard, and my head was still aching. I managed to get the key into the ignition and drove away as fast as the traffic on that horrific street allowed.

CHAPTER 29

I drove down Sheridan Road towards East Winnette till I saw a corner drugstore a few blocks past Devon Avenue. I turned left at the corner and searched for a parking space.

I finally found one and ran all the way to the drugstore. Once I got there, breathing hard, I asked the clerk at the front counter for a phone. "I need to make an important call!" I shouted.

I must have looked borderline psycho because she refused to hand me the drugstore's own phone. Instead she pointed to a pay phone on the back wall.

I ran past racks of toilet paper and feminine products to get to the phone. Luckily I had some change in my wallet. My hands shaking, I somehow managed to call the East Winnette police station and ask for Bob Shakespear.

When Bob got on the line, I didn't say very much. I knew he had to act fast. Jack Hines was going to leave town as soon as he could.

I told Bob about Frank Durkin, too. Jack wasn't too crazy about Frank at the moment, but he might try to reach him and tell him what happened. To save Jack's own skin, if nothing else.

"Jeez, Alison, I'm...I'm really.... I'll get going on this right away," Bob said. "You'd better come by the station before you go home. I'll need more information from you."

I knew I had to show up in person and give Bob the details I'd learned from Jack Hines. I had to pull myself together and get over there as soon as I could.

"Jack hit me," I said, "but I'll try to…."

"He hit you?"

"Don't worry about that right now. Just get a hold of him before he heads out of town."

"I'll tell the Chicago cops to get over there right away," Bob said. "And I'll get some of my own guys to pick up Durkin. I'll see you here as soon as you can make it."

I hung up and threaded my way through the drugstore's racks toward the door. The clerk's startled eyes followed me as I made my hurried escape from the store.

My heart pounding, I headed for the East Winnette police station. The drive seemed to take forever. I hit every red light on the way, my head aching and my hands shaking so violently I could barely hold onto the steering wheel.

I flipped on the car radio and tried to drown out my thoughts with Beethoven on WFMT. But even that didn't help. I tried to keep my eyes on the road, all the way through Evanston to East Winnette.

Once at the station, I rushed inside and asked for Bob. He met me right away and assured me the Chicago police had apprehended Jack Hines just as he was leaving his apartment, carrying his battered suitcase. A couple of East Winnette cops had already taken Frank Durkin in for questioning.

Bob asked me for any details I could muster. I tried to remember what Jack Hines had said. How Kay Boyer had told Frank Durkin that Jack could do some work for Frank in his office. How that led to Frank's hiring Jack to kill Kay.

"God, Alison, we suspected Hines, of course, but we never connected him to anyone else."

"I know."

"And you...you were really gutsy to track Hines down. I hope you realize you took a tremendous risk by going there to confront him like that. No wonder he hit you. You're lucky he didn't do something worse."

"But I didn't view it as a confrontation, Bob. Remember? I just wanted to talk to him, to bask in his admiration and gratitude. I...."

I suddenly remembered Frank's worn leather-bound address book. I still had it in my bag.

Bob interrupted my train of thought.

"Alison, you should get a medal," he said, smiling. "Maybe there's an award like East Winnette Citizen of the Year. I'll personally nominate you."

"Don't be silly, Bob. I was...." Just then I remembered something else. The "order to show cause" I'd found in Frank Durkin's file cabinet.

I didn't want to tell Bob I'd taken it, so I simply said I'd heard that Frank had been served with "an order to show cause" issued by the California medical board. He didn't ask me how I'd learned about it. Maybe he thought my being a lawyer made me privy to that kind of information.

Before he could conjure up any questions, I quickly added that "an order to show cause" could mean Frank had been in some sort of serious trouble. I advised Bob to check it out with the California authorities right away.

"Good idea. I'll do that," he said, jotting down some notes on a scrap of paper.

"One more thing, Bob," I said. "What's happening to Tom Boyer?"

"We're in the process of releasing him. Gotta get through some paperwork first. But the old guy will probably go home in an hour or two."

I wondered what would become of Tom Boyer. Would he be welcomed home by his daughter Bree? I doubted it. But what *would* happen to him?

"Alison," Bob said, interrupting my train of thought again. He was looking carefully at my face. "You look terrible."

Gee, thanks, Bob. But I knew he was right.

"You should go home right now and get some rest. You've done enough for one day."

I returned to the Toyota and slowly drove home. When I got there, the house was quiet. I found a new note on the refrigerator.

Alison:
Took Lindsay to school and went back
to the library to work. Where did you go?
See you later.
M.

I heated up a can of soup and went upstairs to bed. I fell into an exhausted sleep, and when I awoke, the bedroom was dark. I looked over at the clock-radio. 7:30.

My head still hurt.

I washed my face with cold water in an attempt to make my head feel better. When I finally went downstairs, Marv and the girls were seated together on the sofa, looking at their favorite "George and Martha" storybook. I smiled as I listened to Marv reading James Marshall's delightful words.

Missy noticed me first. "Mommy!" she shouted and ran over to me. Lindsay was next. The two of them grabbed me around the hips and screamed with joy. I was just as joyful and relieved to see them.

They finally released their hold on me, and I made my way over to the sofa and Marv. "Thanks for everything you did today," I said, looking into Marv's gray-green eyes.

"What happened to you?" he asked. "Your cheek looks bruised. Are you all right?" The worry on his face was clear. It almost made my head feel better.

"It's a long story," I said. I briefly reviewed the day's events, then changed the subject. I didn't want to think about Kay Boyer or Jack Hines or Frank Durkin anymore. It was up to the police now. I wanted the terrible burden of Kay Boyer's murder to be shifted from my shoulders at last.

I ate some of Marv's leftover pasta while the girls watched, lovingly sitting by my side at the table. They'd missed me, that much was obvious. But I could tell they weren't sure exactly what had happened.

I didn't plan to tell them anytime soon.

I took some Tylenol and went to bed when Missy and Lindsay did. I felt the need for more sleep in spite of all I'd already had. It felt good to escape into my cool quiet bedroom and leave the long ugly day behind.

CHAPTER 30

When I woke up at eight o'clock the next morning, Marv had already fixed breakfast. He seemed harried, rushing around the kitchen, trying to get himself and the girls ready on a morning when he had to teach again.

I helped him get Missy ready for school, then kissed them both goodbye.

Marv gently took my face in his hands. "Take care of yourself, Alison. I don't like what happened yesterday, and I don't want anything else to happen to you," he said. "This job isn't worth your getting hurt like that."

"Okay," I said. "I'll be careful."

"Promise?"

"I promise."

He gave me a hug and went out the door with Missy.

Lindsay and I snuggled up together in the living room with a well-worn "Sesame Street" book. The phone rang a few minutes later.

"Is this Alison?" an ebullient voice asked. "Gabriel Kidd. My secretary tells me you tried to reach me the other day."

"Oh, Mr. Kidd." I'd forgotten all about my call to him.

"Gabriel, please."

"Okay. Gabriel."

"What can I do for you, Alison?"

"Nothing. Not...not anymore," I stammered.

"You did call me, didn't you?"

"Yes," I admitted.

"Well, then...?"

I couldn't tell him I'd suspected him of murder. Not now. "I thought you might want to know Kay Boyer's murder has been solved," I blurted out, saying the first thing that came to mind.

"I already knew that, Alison. They arrested the killer last week."

Right. Gabriel already knew about Jack Hines. "Well, yes, Gabriel, that's the guy who did it, but it turned out he was hired by someone else," I said.

"Oh? Who?"

"Someone named Frank Durkin."

"Durkin?" Gabriel asked. "Who the devil is Durkin?"

"A pediatrician here in East Winnette," I answered. "He and Kay had...had an affair, and when he tried to break it off, she threatened to cause trouble for him. I got the killer to tell me the whole story yesterday."

"But you called me Monday, Alison."

"Oh. That's right, Gabriel." I had to think of some other reason why I'd called him. "I...I was just going to ask you...ask you if you'd thought of anything new that would...that would help me...."

"You didn't think I had anything to do with Kay's death, did you, Alison?" he chided. "I was in a jet thirty thousand feet up when she was killed, or didn't you know that?"

I was silent, and Gabriel resumed speaking. "I spent that Monday night in L.A. and took a direct flight from there to Detroit. It got into Detroit at 9:30 Tuesday morning. You can check with the airline if you like."

"That's not necessary. We know who killed Kay. " I paused. "Please forgive me for even thinking that you might have done it."

"I will, Alison, I will," he said, beginning to laugh. "I do have my problems these days, but I've never considered murder as a solution. Not yet, anyway."

"I'm sure you haven't." I was too embarrassed to say anything else.

"Well, keep in touch, Alison. If you ever want a job in the day-care business, give me a call."

"Thanks. I'll remember that."

Day-care as a career? Never. It was hard enough spending all day with my own kids sometimes. But he was nice to make the offer, I thought. Maybe he could use a lawyer someday...?

"Goodbye now. And good luck!" Gabriel Kidd hung up.

You, too, I thought. You need it.

Lindsay had wandered into the kitchen and pulled out her Play-Doh box. I found her there and was admiring her funny orange-colored shapes when the phone rang again.

"Alison Ross?"

"Yes?" The voice sounded familiar, but I couldn't place it.

"Art Jacoby from the *Tribune*. Can I come by to talk to you this afternoon?"

"Um...I don't think so," I said. I really didn't feel like being interviewed by the press, especially with a bruise still evident on my face.

"Okay. Do you mind if I ask you a few questions now?"

"All right."

"I just talked to the East Winnette police. They tell me you've identified a new killer in the Kay Boyer murder."

"No, he's not a 'new killer,' Art. Jack Hines was the killer all along. But it turns out he did it for money." The press sometimes gets the legal niceties screwed up.

"Okay. And the one who paid him was her lover?"

"Yes," I said. "Well, yes and no. Her lover only promised to pay Jack Hines. He never actually paid him a dime." Another nicety.

"This lover. He's a pediatrician in East Winnette, is that right?"

"Yes," I said.

"What was the motive?"

"Didn't the police tell you?"

"They said something about a quarrel. That right?"

"Yes, that's right," I said. "He wanted to end their affair, and she didn't. She must have threatened to expose his philandering. I guess that was enough to push him over the edge."

"What about the husband?"

"You mean Tom Boyer?"

"Yeah. Didn't he confess, too?"

"Yes, he did," I said. Tom Boyer. He'd confessed to a crime he didn't commit, out of guilt for all the crimes he did.

"Well, what's the story on that?" Art persisted. "I heard he confessed to you yesterday. Then before I could write the piece on it, I got a call that Hines did it after all."

"Look, Art, I can't tell you very much about that right now." I didn't want to reveal the Boyer family's terrible secrets to the press. I hoped no one else would either.

"As far as I can tell, Tom Boyer is a very troubled man," I went on. "I don't understand exactly why he confessed to his wife's murder when he didn't really do it. But I think he felt a lot of guilt for other things he's done over the years. That's all I can say."

I thought again of that revolting old man and the way he'd looked in the nursery school classroom when he confessed to his wife's murder. Although he'd insisted his daughters wanted to go to bed with him, he must have known, in his heart of hearts, that wasn't true. Buried feelings of guilt must have overwhelmed him, leading him to falsely confess to his wife's murder.

Jacoby seemed satisfied and returned to the subject of Jack Hines. "They tell me you got Hines to confess, too. How did that happen?"

I suddenly had an image of Jack Hines's filthy room in the rundown apartment-hotel, replacing the shadowy image of Tom Boyer at the nursery school. I couldn't tell Jacoby about the nightmare I'd lived through in that room.

"I just talked to him, Art. I asked him a few questions, and he spilled the beans pretty fast." I was lying, but I couldn't face describing the details of my meeting with Jack Hines. My head ached just thinking about it.

"That easy, huh? How come the police didn't get him to confess? Didn't they question him?"

Art was right to wonder why the police didn't have more success with Jack Hines. But I knew why. The police had failed to learn very much about Kay Boyer's private life. Thanks to Thelma Eisenmayer's reluctance to talk to the police, they were completely in the dark when it came to Kay's affair with Frank Durkin. And that had been the key to getting Jack Hines to confess.

"Of course they did," I said. "I don't know why they didn't have more success with him. You'd have to ask the police about that." I was being evasive, but I didn't want to reveal how Thelma Eisenmayer had helped me uncover the truth.

"Well, thanks, Alison. Anything else you want to tell me?"

"Not really. Goodbye, Art." I hung up.

I looked around the kitchen and couldn't help noticing how dirty the floor looked. Not much better than the Boyers' kitchen floor. A decapitated doll and a deflated balloon had taken up residence in a dirt-smudged corner. It was clearly time for a hands-and-knees scrubbing again. I'd have to hire a cleaning service to do it; the thought of doing it myself made me feel faint.

Lindsay had wandered back into the living room by now. I was pouring myself a Diet Pepsi, planning to join her, when the doorbell rang. I hurried to the front door and looked through the glass. It was Bob Shakespear, his cherubic face smiling broadly at me. I opened the door and let him in.

"Alison!" he said. "I've been trying to call you, but your line's been busy. So I decided to come over to congratulate you in person."

"Thanks, Bob. Want some coffee?"

"Sure." I led him into the breakfast room and poured the rest of the morning coffee into a mug. We sat down together at the table.

"I still haven't figured out how you did it," he said, shaking his head. "First you got Tom Boyer to confess to the murder, along with a whole string of sex crimes. And yes, Alison, I know you want to keep that part of the story under wraps. Don't worry; I won't reveal it to the press."

I breathed a sigh of relief. Bree Boyer would be spared that, at least.

"But then you turned around and found out it was Jack Hines after all."

I nodded.

"You really had a lot of guts to go down there to talk to that guy," he said. "Why did you do it?"

I thought for a moment. Why *had* I gone off in search of Jack Hines? In retrospect it seemed like a immensely foolish thing to do. But I owed Bob Shakespear an explanation.

"There was something about Tom Boyer's confession that just didn't ring true. He seemed too upset, genuinely upset, by Kay's death to have killed her. Even though I got him to confess, in the last analysis I just couldn't believe he'd murdered her."

I paused for a moment, reviewing once more that morning at the nursery school. "In a way, I think I may have led him to confess. I kept pressing him with questions about what happened. Maybe he decided that if he caved in and admitted killing Kay, he would be absolved of all his sins."

Bob looked dubious. "Do you think he really had a confrontation with Kay over what he'd been doing with their daughters?"

"I don't know. I suppose he did. From what he told me, it seems there was an argument that night. So he may in fact have argued with Kay. But he couldn't have killed her."

"Why not?"

"He was upset and angry and worried about his own future, but I think he still loved Kay. Despite the fact that she'd spurned him for so long. And despite the way he'd turned to his daughters, thinking that they loved him even if she didn't.

"Despite all that, I think he still loved her. Even her accusations, her threats to go to the police, weren't enough to make him kill her. In a way, I think he wanted to be punished for everything...for everything he'd done."

"He did seem to be devastated by her death. That was our reaction to him, too," Bob said. "That's why we never zeroed in on him as a suspect." He looked pleased that his instincts had served him well, at least where Tom Boyer was concerned.

"But what made you suspect Hines," Bob asked, "after all you did to try to clear him? And why, in God's name, did you ever drive over to his apartment alone if you *did* suspect him?"

"But I told you, Bob, I didn't suspect him. Remember? That's not why I went there. I went because I wanted to talk to him. I thought he'd be really glad to see me. After all, I was the one who got him released."

"But there was something else, too," I added.

"Yeah? What was that?"

"The address book."

"Address book? What address book?" Bob looked baffled.

Gulp. I'd forgotten that no one but me–and Frank–knew about the address book. "Frank Durkin's," I said.

"Durkin's address book? How...?"

"I found it."

"Where?"

"In a drawer in Frank's desk."

"What desk?" he asked.

"The one in his study, in his house."

"When was this?" Bob asked.

"Uh, let me see...it must have been Tuesday, or was it Monday?" I stammered. I didn't want this line of questioning to go any further.

Bob didn't push it. "Did the book connect Durkin to Hines?"

I nodded. "Frank had written Jack's address into the book, right under Kay Boyer's phone number. I figured it meant Frank knew Jack Hines, and Frank connected Jack somehow to Kay."

"Jeez, you were right about that," Bob said, taking a last sip from his mug. "Any coffee left?"

"Nope. Sorry. How's a Diet Pepsi?"

He shook his head. "Is the address book still in his desk? I'd like to see it."

"I've got it, Bob," I said quietly. "I can give it to you now if you want it."

Bob looked startled. "You took it from his desk?"

"Umm...," I hesitated. "Let's just say that someone took it from his desk and it's now in my possession." I felt queasy admitting theft to the police, even to Bob Shakespear.

"Well, then, it won't do me any good," he sighed.

"Why not?"

"I can't use illegally obtained evidence. You ought to know that. 'Fruit of the poisonous tree' and all that."

"But the book wasn't taken by a police officer, Bob."

He didn't say anything. I realized I'd just told him something he was supposed to know already.

"Whoever took the book was a private party, Bob. You can use anything I...that person took. The 'fruit of the poisonous tree' rule applies only to evidence obtained by government agents like the police."

Bob nodded. Maybe he'd heard all this before and had simply forgotten it.

"The courts won't automatically exclude evidence collected by other people, even if they took it illegally." I was tempted to tell Bob about an old Illinois precedent, *People v. Touhy,* decided by the Illinois Supreme Court way back in the 1930s. I remembered reading the court's opinion when I worked for Judge Johannsen.

The *Touhy* case stemmed from the kidnapping of an Al Capone-mob character, "Jake the Barber," by members of a warring gang. The court had allowed evidence like Frank's address book to be admitted at trial.

I decided not to embarrass Bob any more than I had to. But I had to admit it felt pretty good to explain the law to him. I felt almost like a practicing lawyer again.

My explanation had also succeeded in distracting him from focusing on my possible role as thief. "Check with the state's attorney's office. I'm sure they'll tell you the same thing," I said.

"I'll do that," Bob said. He rose from the table. "If they tell me it's okay, I'll send someone over for the address book this afternoon."

"I'll be here." We walked together to the front door, and I glanced into the living room. Lindsay was on the sofa, fast asleep. No wonder she hadn't bothered us all this time. I opened the door and walked out onto the porch with Bob.

"There's something else, Alison," he said. "What led you to Frank Durkin in the first place?"

I thought for a moment. Once again, I didn't want to get Thelma Eisenmayer involved if I didn't have to. "I...I got a call, Bob. After my name got in the paper. Someone who used to work for Frank called me."

Knowing that, Bob could probably track down Thelma. I hoped he wouldn't. "She told me about his affair with Kay Boyer."

"Well, it's lucky she did. We might never have connected Durkin to Kay Boyer. The two of them covered their tracks pretty good."

"I guess they did."

It was windy on our screened-in porch, and the big brown leaves descending from our ancient oak tree were blowing through the air, hitting the screens. I looked up at Bob. His gray hair was blowing around, too.

"I almost forgot, Alison!" he said suddenly.

"What?"

"That 'order to show cause' you told me about. The one from California. That turned out to be really important. Once we learned about it, we knew Durkin had real problems."

"What kind of problems? I haven't heard about any of this," I said.

What had I missed, all those hours I spent sleeping?

"Didn't anybody tell you?" He looked surprised I hadn't heard about Frank's problems by this time. But nobody had bothered to tell me.

"It seems that Durkin got in trouble in California about fourteen, fifteen years ago," he said. "He was accused of malpractice when two babies died after what looked like gross negligence on his part. After the parents alerted the medical licensing board, the board began to look into our Dr. Durkin. It had just begun proceedings to suspend his license to practice when he disappeared."

"Disappeared?"

"He apparently packed up and left in the middle of the night. He and his family wound up back here. He'd gone to medical school in Chicago, and he'd been a resident at a Chicago hospital before moving to California. He already had a license to practice here, so he just set up practice in East Winnette without telling anybody what happened in California."

"My God," I said. "And no one ever found out about it?"

It was shocking to think that a doctor could leave one state and move to another, with no repercussions arising from medical negligence. The people in charge of professional records had done a reprehensible job back in the '60s, allowing Frank to slip through the cracks like that. I wondered whether professional record-keeping had improved at all since then.

"Someone did find out about it," Bob said. "Kay Boyer."

Kay Boyer. Of course.

Now I understood. *That* was why Frank wanted her killed.

He didn't care if she talked about their love affair. He probably enjoyed his reputation as a womanizer. She could have gone to the *National Enquirer* and all the other scandal-soaked tabloids, and he wouldn't have done a damned thing about it. But this...this was something else.

"How did she find out?"

"Once we heard from California, we told Durkin we knew Kay Boyer had found out about it. We were bluffing, of course, but he didn't know that, and even with his lawyer there, he spilled his guts.

"He said she was the type who wanted to know everything about him. She was always asking him details about his past— where he'd lived, where he'd gone to school, who he knew, that kind of thing. Somehow the story slipped out. He said she was sympathetic about it at first. She even cried when he told her about the babies who died. But when their affair started turning sour, she began throwing his past up to him and threatening to talk about it. That's when he started looking for a way out."

It was clear, very clear now. Frank had been telling the truth when he said he didn't care if people knew he had affairs. But he didn't want anyone to know the ugly truth about his professional negligence, about the two babies who had died in California.

I wondered briefly how those babies had died. But I didn't really want to know.

"Well, thanks again for all your help, Alison," Bob was saying. "I've gotta run. Can I buy you lunch sometime?"

"Sure," I said. "Any day you like, as long as it's after 12:30. That's when Lindsay goes to school."

"Right. I'll give you a call. Maybe over a hamburger you can tell me the secret to success as a detective." He laughed.

I said goodbye and watched Bob walk down the front steps. He climbed into his unmarked car and drove off, dry autumn leaves swirling around the car as it disappeared from sight.

CHAPTER 31

Once Bob Shakespear left, I found Lindsay upstairs, play-ing with the dollhouse in her bedroom. I was grateful she'd been happily preoccupied while Bob and I had talked on the porch.

After we both munched on melted cheese sandwiches and carrot sticks for lunch, I dropped her off at school.

It felt strange, watching her walk into the classroom where, a day before, Tom Boyer had lied to me and told me that he killed his wife. Where, just over a week ago, I'd found Kay's body in the blood-soaked chest of old clothes. I forced myself to forget all that and drove home to face the pile of dirty laundry in the basement.

I sank into the sofa and tried to relax before hitting the laundry room. Just then, I heard noises at the back door. It couldn't be Marv. He never got home on Thursdays till close to dinnertime.

Was there someone trying to break into the house? The back door always seemed terribly vulnerable to me. Marv had installed a deadbolt lock a year before, but I still didn't feel entirely safe.

Now, my pulse suddenly racing, I rose from the sofa and walked shakily toward the breakfast room, wondering whether everything I'd been up to during the past week had made me a target. The chosen victim of some pscho killer who'd read about me in the *Tribune*.

But instead of a killer, there was Marv, looking through his briefcase.

I could finally breathe. "Hi, darling. You're home early," I said.

"The power went out in my office, so I couldn't get any work done there. Thought I'd try to work here instead," he said. He was gazing at me with concern. "How are you feeling, sweetness?"

"I'm much better," I said. "And I'm glad you're home. I've been wanting to tell you everything that's happened. There just hasn't been a good time to do it."

He put his things away, and we walked into the living room together. "Tell me," he said, taking my hand in his as we sat down on the sofa.

I told Marv everything, from Thelma Eisenmayer and Frank Durkin, to the revelations about Kay Boyer and her tragically messed-up family. Marv soaked up every detail, and I could see his mathematician's mind fitting everything together.

"Your figuring out that Jack Hines was the real killer was brilliant, sweetness."

"Not so brilliant," I said, pointing at my bruised cheek. "Look what I have to show for it."

Marv gave me a rueful smile. "I wish you hadn't gone through that ordeal at his apartment. And I hope you *never* go through anything like that again. But...if you hadn't done it, no one would ever know what really happened."

"True."

"Tom Boyer's role here was bizarre, wasn't it? Listening to his confession must have been rough."

I nodded. The image of Tom's weirdly grief-stricken face suddenly appeared in my brain. "Why do you think he confessed to me like that?"

Marv paused. "You think he confessed to killing Kay out of guilt, right?"

"Right."

"And the guilt stemmed from…?"

"From the abuse he inflicted on his daughters."

Marv was silent, considering all of the facts, putting them together in his unfailingly logical brain.

"What are you thinking?" I asked.

"I agree that Tom may have felt some degree of guilt for the way he treated his daughters. But didn't he claim that his daughters loved him, that they wanted to be close to him?" Marv said.

"Yes."

"And didn't he say that Kay had begun to ignore him, that he looked to his daughters for the love that was missing in his marriage?"

"Yes…."

"Then I think something else was going on here."

"Something else?"

"Everything you've said makes sense, sweetness. But I don't think Tom confessed to killing Kay simply because he felt guilty about his daughters. It's more complicated than that."

This was going to be interesting.

"My guess is that Tom still harbored a deep love for Bree," Marv continued. "Deeper than his love for Kay. When Kay confronted him that night, throwing accusations at him, he probably got angry. Angry with Kay. But he also learned it was Bree who told Kay what happened."

"Right."

"When she confronted Tom, Kay may have told him she and Bree had argued. She may have even said that Bree resented her for never coming to Bree's rescue."

Yes, that was possible.

"If I'm right," Marv said, "Tom still loved Bree. In his twisted mind, he may have jumped to the conclusion that Bree hated Kay. Hated her enough to harm her."

"So...?"

"So when he learned that someone had killed Kay, his warped mind may have taken him one step further. Remember, although the police arrested Jack Hines, no one was sure he was the real killer. You were planting doubts about him in a lot of people's minds."

"I guess I was...."

"So when Tom got wind of the idea that Jack Hines might not have killed Kay after all, he may have panicked and thought Bree was the real killer."

"I thought Bree was a possible suspect myself," I said.

"That's right. You did. So you can see why Tom might have reached the same conclusion."

"So when I talked to Tom that morning at the nursery school, he...?"

"He must have been filled with anxiety, thinking that Bree had caused Kay's death."

"He did seem terribly anxious. But I thought he was anxious because he'd killed Kay. I might have even pushed him to confess, Marv. I think I put words in his mouth, encouraging him to admit killing Kay."

"But that wasn't what compelled him to confess."

"It wasn't?"

"No," Marv said. "Above all, Tom was worried that the blame would fall on Bree. He still loved Bree, and he confessed to protect her. He chose to be viewed as Kay's killer rather than see Bree accused of murder."

Marv was right. It all fell into place. Kay had confronted Tom, just as Bree had asked her to. Kay was wildly upset, but she was still unsure that Bree was telling her the truth.

Kay must have told Tom she suspected that Bree had seduced him. That she and Bree had a violent argument as a result.

Tom brooded over her words all night, waking up to learn that Kay was dead. And to fear that Bree was her killer.

When I questioned him that morning in the darkened classroom, he was worried about Bree. Then and there, he concocted his phony story to protect her.

I turned to Marv and gave him an enormous hug. "You're a better detective than I am, darling," I said. "It never occurred to me that Tom was worried about Bree and wanted to protect her."

"No, sweetness, you're the real detective here. You uncovered all the facts in this case. I never would have met up with Thelma Eisenmayer and Gabriel Kidd, or searched Durkin's house, or sought out Jack Hines, alone, at his apartment.

"And you put it all together exactly right," Marv added. "Don't forget, you solved the case when you came across that order to show cause and realized how crucial it could be. I never would have known the meaning of a legal document like that."

"You know what I think?" I said, a smile spreading over my face.

"What?"

"We make a pretty good team, you and me."

Marv smiled back. "Just let me know the next time there's a murder in East Winnette. We'll put our heads together and come up with the killer on the spot."

"Deal," I said.

"And now, sweetness, I have to get some work done." Marv picked up his briefcase where he'd left it and sat down at the breakfast table to begin grading papers.

I knew it was time to leave Marv to his work. I wanted to call Judy and tell her everything, but I couldn't put off the laundry any longer. I'd call Judy later.

I was about to descend to the laundry room and the pile of dirty clothes when the phone rang. I grabbed the living room phone before it disturbed Marv.

"Is this Mrs. Ross?" A woman's voice. It sounded familiar.

"Yes."

"This is Elmira Hines."

Oh, God. I'd forgotten all about her. What could I possibly say to this woman? She'd hired me to help her son, and I'd done the exact opposite. Instead of exonerating him, I'd gotten him to confess to murder.

"I have something to say to you," she said. I prepared myself for the worst. A harsh scolding, a blistering attack on me and on everything I'd done to condemn her son to imprisonment, maybe death.

"I...I want to thank you," she said.

Thank me? Was this some kind of joke?

"I know you tried to help my Jack, and I don't blame you for nothing."

I wasn't sure what to say.

"Look, Jack was a troublemaker ever since he was a kid," she went on. "I did the best I could, but nothing I did made any difference. He was just a bad kid from the start."

My heart went out to Elmira Hines. It had to be immensely difficult to admit you've produced a bad child. I hoped I'd never have to make that kind of admission.

"I did try to help him," I said.

"I know. The police told me. And I want you to know I appreciate it."

"I'm glad you understand what happened." I suddenly remembered the smudged envelope in the dining room sideboard. "But don't worry, I'll send your forty dollars back to you. I'll put it in the mail this afternoon."

"Oh, no," she said. "I want you to keep that money."

"I can't keep it. Not now."

"Oh, yes, you can. You keep that money. You earned it."

I'd earned it all right. I'd done everything I could to help Jack Hines, and he'd repaid me in spades. I had a puffy, bruised face to prove it. But I couldn't let his mother pay me for tying a rope around his neck.

"I really can't keep...."

"Mrs. Ross, if you send that money back to me, I'll just send it back to you again. It's your money, and I won't hear any more about it." She hung up.

I replaced the receiver and thought for a moment. Elmira Hines was right. Any self-respecting detective would keep a fee paid in a case like this. I'd done my job. I'd tried to find out who killed Kay Boyer. And if it turned out that Jack Hines did it after all, well, that wasn't my fault.

I'd keep the money. I *had* earned it. I'd earned a fee, the first money I'd earned in a while. It felt good.

I remembered the mountain of laundry in the basement and headed downstairs. I was pre-spotting some kid-sized Levi's when I thought I heard the phone ring again. I ran upstairs to get it before Marv did.

"Hello, Alison!" a familiar voice boomed.

"Hello," I answered, not completely sure who it was.

"It's Dick Johanssen! Remember me?"

Was he kidding? You don't easily forget the judge who gave you your first job after law school, the judge you worked with closely for two exciting years, the judge who helped mold you into something you wanted to be—a good lawyer.

"Judge Johanssen! What a wonderful surprise!"

"Haven't heard from you in a long time. Why not?"

"I...I've been busy at home, Judge. I don't get downtown much these days."

"Busy with your family, am I right? When are you going to go back to the law? We need more good lawyers like you," he said. "I ought to know."

"I'm not sure, Judge. Soon, I think." What else could I say?

"Well, Alison, I'll tell you why I called," he said. "A fellow from the *Tribune* just called me. Wanted to know if I had any comments on your solving a murder out in East Winnette. I didn't know what to say till he explained what happened. I hadn't heard anything about it."

"I just got the murderer to confess yesterday."

"Well, Alison, I told the fellow I wasn't a bit surprised that you solved this murder. You were a real crackerjack when you worked for me."

"Thanks, Judge."

"You really must go back to work one of these days."

"Oh, yes, I plan to," I assured him.

"The only question now is: Will you be a lawyer–or a detective?" Judge Johanssen laughed heartily at his own joke. He always did.

I laughed too, and we said our goodbyes. But when I hung up, the question lingered in my mind.

I had to admit that I liked being a detective. I felt good about discovering what had really happened to Kay Boyer, about solving a crime after the police had nearly botched it. It would be exciting to do that again sometime.

But I'd also loved being a lawyer. The consultations with clients in need of my help, the plunge into the library to find precedents that would bolster my case, the arguments in court that led to rulings in my favor...all that could be heady stuff. And I missed it sometimes.

I glanced over at Lindsay's Play-Doh shapes, still lying where she'd left them. Sure, it would be exciting to be a full-time detective who took on cases like this one. And returning to the full-time practice of law would probably be as rewarding as I remembered.

No doubt I'd end up doing one or the other someday. But in the meantime I had a couple of years to go at home. I wanted to be there just a little bit longer.

To be the principal influence on my children, to be someone they could always rely on, instead of turning that job over to somebody else.

I knew I wouldn't be happy doing anything else, at least for a while.

Those dirty Levi's in the basement called out to me, and I headed for the basement stairs to face them.

Of course, I thought as I descended the stairs, if a good part-time job came along...that would be a different story.

AUTHOR'S NOTE

I wrote the original version of this story when I was "between jobs" (part-time jobs, of course) in the fall of 1985. At that time, I was still close enough to 1981 to pattern the backdrop in *Jealous Mistress* after my life at that time.

In this story, I've tried to capture the dilemma faced by women lawyers during that era. Those who married and had children had to make difficult choices. The legal profession was not receptive to women (or men) who wanted to achieve a balance between work and family. Young lawyers were expected to work long hours as they ascended the law-firm ladder, and the profession offered few opportunities to work less than full-time. Women like me, who loved much about being a lawyer but also wanted to spend time with my family, generally had to sacrifice the goal of a high-profile legal career.

Before my children were born, I thought it would be easy to turn them over to others while I pursued my career, but once they appeared on the scene, my thinking changed. I felt a gravitational pull to be with my children while they were young. In an effort to achieve a balance between work and family, I constantly attempted to find interesting and meaningful part-time work. Although that presented a daunting challenge during most of the '70s and '80s, I was often successful. Between jobs, I spent much of my time on freelance writing.

The situation has shifted considerably during the past 30 years. As the number of women lawyers has escalated, the legal profession has undergone dramatic changes, and both women and men have more choices now. But I continue to learn of lawyers, especially women lawyers, who abandon the law out of a frustration with its demands. It seems that the goal of balancing work as a lawyer with the role of parent continues to be a struggle for many.

Regarding the locations and characters in *Jealous Mistress*: Although some of the locations I describe may seem familiar to those who have spent time in the North Shore suburbs of Chicago, with a few exceptions they do not depict any real places.

In addition, although the characters I created may resemble some of those who inhabited my life in 1981, for the most part they are not based on any real individuals but are composites of many people I knew.

The only characters in the story who depict real people in any way are Alison's husband Marv, Alison's two young daughters, and Alison herself.

Like Alison, in 1981 I was a graduate of Harvard Law School who decided to forgo a high-profile legal career and, while my two daughters were young, spend most of my time with my family. But, also like Alison, I was always in pursuit of a good part-time job. Although there are therefore many parallels between Alison's life and mine, this is a work of fiction, and my life story was not exactly like Alison's.

The character of Marv may strike some readers as an idealized husband, one who's too good to be true, but he's based on my late husband, Herb Alexander. Herb was in truth very much like Marv (and he really did call me "sweetness"). Herb gave me boundless love and support as I wrote this book and throughout our wonderful marriage, which ended much too soon.

The events described in this book are totally fictional.

ABOUT THE AUTHOR

Susan Alexander is a graduate of Harvard Law School who has worked as a lawyer in the public interest and has also served as a federal judge's law clerk, an arbitrator, a law school professor, and a consultant on legal writing. She also worked at three Chicago law firms. She earned her A.B. with highest honors from Washington University in St. Louis and an M.A. in political science from Northwestern University.

Susan now focuses primarily on writing. Her writing has appeared in a wide array of publications, including the San Francisco Chronicle, the Chicago Tribune, the Chicago Sun-Times, The San Francisco Daily Journal, the Chicago Daily Law Bulletin, and a host of other professional and mainstream publications. She was the first editor of *The Almanac of the Federal Judiciary,* and her short story "Neglect" was a winner in *Chicago Lawyer* magazine's first annual fiction competition.

Susan Alexander lives in San Francisco. Her first novel, *A Quicker Blood,* was published in 2009. *Jealous Mistress* is her second novel. Visit her website at www.susanalexander.com.

Made in the USA
Las Vegas, NV
01 February 2022